Kate sat, loathing Jubal Peach, hating his greed, his smirk, his threats, his seductions, his obsession with having it all, locking up all the games in town, destroying her if she resisted.

"Anaway," he said, "when you make a statement you got to make me believe it. I never looked down the bore of a cannon."

Kate slid her hand to a small shelf below the board and clasped her derringer. She whipped it up and pointed it steadily at Peach's heart.

"Now do you believe it?" she asked softly.

It took him a minute to respond. Then he smiled. "You wouldn't."

She brought the derringer up again and cocked it.

DEUCES
AND
LADIES
WILD

Richard S. Wheeler

FAWCETT GOLD MEDAL • NEW YORK

A Fawcett Gold Medal Book
Published by Ballantine Books
Copyright © 1991 by Richard Wheeler

Library of Congress Catalog Card Number: 91-91838

ISBN 0-449-14710-X

Manufactured in the United States of America

First Edition: July 1991

Chapter 1

The blare of martial music drifted faintly through the window, barely disturbing Santiago Toole's concentration. The doctor was attempting to duplicate some of the techniques developed by Robert Koch. The great German bacteriologist had learned how to use aniline dyes to stain bacteria, making them visible under a microscope.

Dr. Toole smeared a fine stain of purple dye across his glass slide with satisfaction, and waited a moment for the soft autumnal breeze billowing the window curtains to dry his work. The music grew louder. It seemed melancholy, a brass-band dirge. He wondered idly what on earth occasioned a brass band on an August afternoon in Miles City, Montana Territory. Briefly he ran through the holidays these Americans kept, Fourth of July and Thanksgiving being the ones he'd known nothing of in Kilkenny.

Sighing, he set his glass slide aside and donned his black frock coat with the steel star pinned to its lapel. The procession, whatever it celebrated, was marching west on Main Street a block to the south, and perhaps that was sheriff's business. He'd better have a quick look, anyway. That's how it went: whenever he was deep in medical pursuits, his sheriff vocation intruded. And whenever he was busy with law enforcement matters, medical emergencies cropped up. He wondered briefly why he stuck with the two vocations, and knew at once the answer: Medicine alone netted him two or three hundred dollars plus a few chickens and a lot of pious promises.

1

His pursuit of the elusive streptococcus would have to wait. He poked around his frame cottage looking for Mimi, and didn't find her. No matter. People looking for a doctor had no trouble finding Santiago Toole in a town of a thousand.

He stepped into the bright sun and blinked, feeling the instant heat of it on his black trousers, frock coat, and vest. He went unarmed into the lazy afternoon, though he usually hoisted a revolver to his waist for his morning and evening rounds. Afternoon was when he practiced medicine, and he always trusted no hooligan would have the effrontery to disturb it.

He paced easily toward Main Street, and arrived just in time to see the Miles City Odd Fellows Band in red plumage proceeding westward. A parade? Surely someone would have told the sheriff. But that didn't puzzle him so much as the next sight that affronted his unbelieving eyes. A hearse. Indeed, such a hearse as Miles City had never seen. Driven by Sylvane Tobias, arrayed in black stovepipe hat and gloomy countenance.

Santiago gaped and hurried closer.

This was a hearse to do justice to kings and presidents and admirals. It rolled over the rutted clay of Main Street looking like it didn't belong there, an ebony apparition that amazed the eye. The entire carriage had been lacquered black and shone in the sun like a dark dream. Its nickel trim glared and glinted. At the belly of the carriage, surrounded by the spoked wheels, was a windowed compartment, each oval pane of beveled glass supplying a view of the burden within. Two black pompoms resolutely announced the presence of death. And there in the bowels of the hearse, visible to all through those cut-glass windows, rested a dark and costly casket, burdened with a black wreath and surrounded by bright asters.

But no one had died! Santiago was sure of it. It didn't seem possible for death to escape the man who was not only the town's doctor but also its sheriff. Nonetheless, there was Tobias, solemnly steering his two clopping drays, the big black gelding named Hell and the dappled gray Purgatory, westward toward the edge of Miles and south to the growing cemetery high on the bluffs.

The brass band and its dirges had attracted the whole of Miles City, and Santiago spotted merchants and customers boiling out of mercantiles, barbers and half-shorn customers erupting onto the new boardwalks, milliners and ranch women gaping. Santiago trotted behind the black apparition, more curious than ever. He remembered now that Tobias had ordered the hearse. It had had to be shipped clear from Sioux City by riverboat and train.

Santiago, as doctor and sheriff, delighted in cheating his friend Sylvane Tobias out of business, but rowdy Miles City yielded up its dead in spite of Toole's best efforts, and here was one Santiago hadn't heard about. A knot of blue-bloused soldiers from Fort Keogh paused under a porch overhang to watch the show. For that's what this was, Santiago thought. A show. Death was this day's entertainment.

The ebony-and-nickel carriage wobbled through deep ruts, the flowers within its chamber swaying behind the glass. Santiago hastened forward until he got full abreast of the carriage, and that's when he saw the small discreet sign through the oval cut-glass windows: JUBAL PEACH. Someone, Tobias presumably, had lettered the cardboard neatly. Jubal Peach!

Impossible! thought Santiago. As of late last night Jubal Peach had been skinning pilgrims and swaddies at his faro layout in The Buffalo Hump Celebrity Hall. Jubal Peach! Holy Mary, how could that be? But there was the late Jubal Peach, encased in a gleaming black casket mounded with flowers, being slowly drawn to his last resting place by old Sylvane.

Some wild flare of suspicion lanced Santiago. Had Peach been shot—certainly an occupational hazard in his trade—and were they all rushing the remains out to the little cemetery up on the Yellowstone River bluffs to keep the sheriff from discovering bullet holes—and a crime? Should he disrupt this solemn funeral and demand to see the late and unloved victim? Irritably he paced beside the black carriage, wondering what to do. He trotted around to the other side and discovered an identical sign propped up behind the oval, beveled-glass windows on that side. Odd that Peach's passage to wherever he was going—Santiago knew it was downslope to nether regions—was so lightly treated by the curious denizens of Miles City. For here was an oddity: Scarcely a grieving face did he spot among the gawking spectators. Not that any of them would shed a tear for the likes of Jubal Peach, but death itself is sad and solemn, and decent people respect the departed.

As the hearse wobbled down the wide clay street it drew a great crowd behind it, as a hay wagon draws horses. Raucous children, impolite in the presence of death. Young clerks with sleeve garters. Horton Gatz, bald owner of Gatz Mercantile and Hardware, peering through rimless glasses, sucked along by the commotion. Santiago hurried, too, his astonishment building as the solemn parade pierced into the West End, that famous quarter where saloons stood cheek-by-jowl, catering to swaddies from the fort, railroad men, and in recent years cowboys, some from as far as that infernal place called Texas. Santiago had the urge to shoo the young hellions away from this tenderloin part of Miles bordered by Main and Sixth Street and Park, but he saw at once he'd never succeed. Half of Miles City now trailed the awesome new squeak-wheeled hearse and its sad burden. Sun lancing from its nickel fittings dazzled his eyes.

They passed the Cosmopolitan Theater and Saloon at Sixth, then the Buffalo Hump, and at once hard-eyed men in soiled white aprons and collarless shirts collected around its Main Street side door, watching with unblinking stares. Now, there was another oddity. Why hadn't the Buffalo Hump shut down in respect for its owner? And why weren't these saloonkeepers and sports and toughs joining the mourners heading out to plant Jubal Peach?

Santiago resolved to get to the bottom of it. He wouldn't halt these solemn proceedings, but afterward he intended to find out exactly how and when Jubal Peach had expired, and if necessary exhume the remains. There might be a murder in it, he thought grimly. Peach had pushed and bulled his way to the top of the Miles City sporting fraternity. He owned all the faro, roulette, monte, and poker tables in the Buffalo Hump, as well as seven other saloons and sporting palaces. In fact he dominated the entire gambling life of Miles City, with one notable exception—the faro layout run by Miss Kate.

Various of the sports and plug-uglies did join the throng, marching with boozy breath and dusty derbies out south of town, almost at the Tongue River, where a two-rut road curled up onto a windy bench land where Miles City planted its dead. No one talked. The planting of a late citizen was not an occasion for banter, even if the late citizen was Jubal Peach.

Jubal had come from the South somewhere, where he had gotten in trouble with the Confederate Army for some reason, spending his military career starving in a stockade. When he'd blown into Miles two years earlier, about when the cowboys were turning Miles into their northern Paris, Santiago had done some discreet checking. He liked to know what there was to know about the town's sports and low-lifes. The sallow, baggy-eyed, black-haired gent with the black goatee and waxed-tip mustache had instantly interested him. Toole had gone over to the telegrapher, Fortney Clewes, at the Northern Pacific station and had sent an inquiry to General David Cook of the Rocky Mountain Detective Association, the splendid and discreet private agency that kept track of such matters, and learned nothing. No record of any sort. But that didn't mean anything. Santiago hadn't even known if Jubal Peach was his real name.

Within months Peach was king of the West End. He whispered softly and with a southern slur, outwardly reserved and secretive and poised, and yet an army of his toughs had spread out into the neighboring saloons and had bought layouts or driven their owners out of business one way or another, always somehow narrowly within the law as far as Santiago could determine. Peach had sent genteel gifts—even a blooded horse once—which Toole had politely refused. Peach built a gingerbreaded tan-brick mansion overlooking the restless river, and had lived in style with a shadowy lady friend people rarely saw.

On one occasion Peach had summoned Dr. Toole to his bedside. Bilious fever had been the complaint. Toole had been shown in by a gaunt blond woman, led through a richly furnished house with heavy brocaded shades drawn against offending sunlight and fresh air, to a room where the king of Miles City sports lay in a walnut four-poster, looking feverish and deathly ill. Beside him on a nightstand stood an amazing array of patent medicines. Santiago had scanned them all, hoping to get an inkling of Peach's maladies. Among them, Dr. Sage's Catarrh Remedy. Dalley's Magical Pain Extractor. Pe-ru-na. Quaker Bitters for dyspepsia and blood. Wild Cherry Tonic. Dr. Parmenter's Magnetic Oil for rheumatism. Dr. D. Jayne's Alternative, for scrofula (king's evil), white swellings, cancerous and indolent tumors, mercurial and syphilitic afflictions. rheumatism, gout, scurvy . . .

Santiago had diagnosed ague and had dosed the gambler with three-grain tablets of sulphate of quinine. A lot of southerners seemed to have ague, which pounced on them intermittently. Peach had gone through the classic cold stage, shivering, his hands and feet icy, his respiration rapid, his stomach nauseated. Then the hot stage, feverish and dry, with pronounced thirst. Peach had proceeded to the sweating stage by the time Santiago got there, and lay drenched in his sheets. Santiago eyed his new patient contemplatively. Old-time doctors supposed ague was caused by "miasmas," poisonous gases rising from swamps and decaying vegetation, but Santiago doubted it.

"It interferes with business," muttered Peach in his odd whispery voice. "How long will I be abed?"

"I can't say," Santiago had replied. "But you'd be foolish to go back to your tables too soon. You need fresh air and sunlight."

Jubal Peach had smiled crookedly. "Here's a dollar for your services, and I'll have them serve you a free whiskey."

"I charge two, plus two more for the quinine."

"You take money from helpless people sick abed. I take

money from the sports. Two of a kind, Toole, two of a kind.
There's a stack of house chips. Help yourself, and may you
lose.''

Santiago had pocketed three, plus the dollar.

And now Peach was dead. The fact of it aroused every
sort of suspicion in Santiago Toole.

The silent crowd, half of Miles City by now, puffed its
way up the steep slope behind the wobbling hearse. Santiago
noticed sports from the Buffalo Hump, barmen with hair
parted in the middle, three aging waitresses with curling-
iron hair, leathery white faces, and varicose veins at their
exposed ankles, several table men with brocaded waistcoats
and string ties and pearly-gray frock coats. So they'd come
after all, he thought. He planned to question some when this
was over.

The big black hearse negotiated the hairpin at the top and
rattled easterly into the cemetery, its destination a plush black
canopy lodged in the Odd Fellows quarter. A first-class funeral, Santiago thought. A fancy hearse, a band, a velvety
black canopy staked over the grave. The swelling crowd
boiled around the deep hole in the yellow clay and peered
in, transfixed. The sports from the Buffalo Hump crowded
around a carved walnut headboard lying at the head of the
grave. JUBAL PEACH, it said. And underneath, KING OF
MILES CITY. And the dates, 1836–1882.

Sylvane Tobias descended slowly from the seat of his shiny
conveyance, eyed Santiago coldly, and proceeded to dust off
himself and his black stovepipe carefully. Santiago peered
about, wanting to discover a minister in this mob, but found
none. Well, he thought, that made sense. Peach was not a
man for ministers.

With quiet dignity Tobias walked around to the rear of the
hearse and opened the ornate black-lacquered door, which
swung on its nickel-plated hinges. Sylvane seemed unusually
solemn, Santiago thought, considering what he privately
thought of Jubal Peach, an opinion he had expressed vehe-
mently and frequently to the sheriff in the confines of his
cabinetmaking shop. But Tobias's solemnity had the glare of

money about it, and Santiago understood perfectly. For a fancy planting like this Sylvane Tobias would be as solemn as a widow-and-orphan lawyer.

Tobias nodded politely, expecting pallbearers to emerge from the mob and help him. But no one did. The sports from the Buffalo Hump simply stood rooted to earth. Odd, Santiago thought. Very odd.

"Dr. Toole," said Sylvane. "I will seek your assistance. And you and you," he added, pointing to the two cornet players, the trombonist, and the tuba player of the Odd Fellows Band. The fat snare drummer looked relieved, for some reason. Nonetheless, the four set down their brass instruments and helped Tobias and Toole ease the heavy burnished-walnut casket out of the hearse and set it on three webbed canvas straps. With these they lowered the gloomy burden into the yellow hole, sweating slightly even in the brown shade of the canopy.

Sylvane Tobias quietly assumed a place at the head of the grave and doffed his silken top hat, revealing a mane of white that framed his ruddy square face. The mob did likewise, at least those who wore hats, and pressed those felt hats and blue fatigue army hats to their breasts.

Tobias blinked and cleared his throat. "We've come to pay our respects to a premier citizen of Miles City, and a great and fine gentleman," began Tobias.

Sheriff Toole listened, faintly astonished.

"The Honorable Jubal Peach grew up, I understand, in Hattiesburg, Mississippi, scion of a great plantation owner and cotton magnate. Mr. Peach grew to adulthood in the bosom of a loving family that cherished Scriptures and observed the Sabbath, and treated its slaves gently except when they ran away. Even at an early age it was said of this young man that he had a noble bearing, an inviolate heart, a soul that was a model of rectitude, and a keen business acumen, which he perfected at poker and mockingbird-hunting and alligator-wrestling."

The sports from the Buffalo Hump stared flint-eyed, and Tobias resumed his eulogy. "After the late War of the Rebellion, Mr. Peach left the bosom of his beloved family to engage in his own enterprises. The plantation lay in ruins, the victim of war, and his dear parents lay deep beneath the fertile loam of their lost lands. Mr. Peach swiftly recouped the family fortune, settling large estates on his two surviving sisters, who regrettably can't be with us this sad day. Mr. Peach became a capitalist, undertaking business ventures on the Mississippi River in the shipping services field, and eventually bringing his light and enterprise and wisdom to this remote corner of the world. He's blessed Miles City with no fewer than seven business establishments, thereby greatly enhancing the local economy. And of course he built the finest residence in the territory yonder on the slopes, a residence befitting the grandeur of his vision. He proved in the building of it that he had come to stay and contribute his great business skills to this thriving new community.''

The crowd listened quietly, holding hats to breasts and feeling the heat of the sun on their bared heads.

''Now, the Honorable Jubal Peach was a freethinker, having come to that opinion in recent years through ceaseless examination and questioning of Scriptures, and for that reason we will not offer him a Christian burial here, though I must say that throughout his life he practiced a personal saintliness that all of us here now remember and honor and esteem.

''So we shall say good-bye, hail and farewell, to this fine and blessed entrepreneur. May our fair city remember him! Indeed, in the years to come, the good citizens of Miles City will come to remember Jubal Peach as one of the Founding Fathers, gracious to a fault. And so we bury him now. Let us remember Jubal Peach with a moment of silence, before we depart.''

Santiago's moment of silence turned dizzy with protestation. Was Sylvane Tobias mad? Had he taken leave of his senses? But gradually Santiago understood: speak no ill of the dead, he remembered, though he couldn't recollect the original Latin motto. Good, generous Sylvane was speaking no ill.

A few moments later Toole was still standing quietly on the windswept promontory, feeling the air rushing through his black worsted clothes, while the great mob solemnly dissolved and trudged down the long rutted slope to the city. No one had said a word. The red-tuniced, gold-braided band plucked up its brass and lumbered down the hill. Santiago stood, staring at the coffin that lay darkly in its hole, until at last Tobias's two grave-diggers began shoveling clay over it, making it boom and rattle as the clods of earth hit it.

Sylvane said nothing.

"Would you explain this?" Santiago asked. "When did he die? Why the haste? Why wasn't I summoned? Was he injured?"

Sylvane Tobias sighed, doffed his silk hat, and stared at Santiago through somber blue eyes. "Later, Santiago. Not now. Let me finish my tasks here. Then we'll palaver."

"At least tell me what Peach died of, and when," Santiago insisted. "I have to know."

"Later."

"This cost a pretty penny. Who paid?"

"Later, Santiago."

Irritably, Sheriff Toole gave up. Let the man finish his burying, dismantle the canopy, and drive that awesome black thing he'd just bought down to town.

Santiago left them at their labors and walked alone down to Miles, pondering each and every possibility. Shot? Sylvane would have said something. Cholera or some fast death? A medical panic, and he'd have been called at once. Cardiovascular? Perhaps. But why the rush? Drunk? Opiated? Poisoned? Unlikely. Murdered by that gaunt blond woman? Something to check out.

With a wave of irritation at Tobias boiling through him Santiago stalked angrily into town, bee-lining straight toward The Buffalo Hump Celebrity Hall, which stood false-fronted and whitewashed in afternoon glory. He'd start by collaring half of the help there—in fact, all of the help—and get the story.

He barged in and stood just inside the swinging doors,

letting his eyes adjust to the gloom, smelling whiskey and stale beer and lamp oil. At last he could see. Not a patron loitered in Peach's place. But there, before Santiago's eyes, chewing on a greasy cigar, lounging in his usual spot behind a fancy faro layout and looking mean, sat Jubal Peach.

Chapter 2

There stood Toole, surprise all over his face. Jubal Peach smiled faintly. The sheriff would ask questions, of course. Peach wondered what to tell him, if anything. He settled for nothing.

The sheriff recovered his wits and approached, incredulous.

"It's you."

"No other," replied Peach. "Try your luck, eh?"

"No thanks. I have some questions."

"Try your luck."

Santiago Toole stared sourly at the faro layout, pulled a greenback from his pocket, and purchased four chips.

"That's better," said Peach. "Business is business."

Toole knew that, of course. Everyone knew it. No one, not a soul other than his own people, ever talked with Jubal Peach without doing a little business. Peach calculated it brought him an extra three or four hundred a year from people who never went near a sporting layout. He shuffled methodically, let Toole cut, and dropped the cards into the case box. He pulled the soda, a trey of clubs. The green oilcloth had the whole spade suit painted on it in black. Dourly Santiago placed a chip on the seven. Peach pulled a six of hearts, loser, and eight of diamonds, winner. The case-keeper, sitting at Peach's right, flipped the beads on the abacus-like contraption before him. Peach smiled.

"Did you do that?" Santiago asked.

"Do what?"

12

"Have yourself planted?"

Peach smiled, drew the ten of clubs, loser, and seven of diamonds, winner. Lazily he added a chip to Santiago's.

"There, you see, Toole? You've won."

Santiago yanked the spare chip off the board, obviously intending to make his dollar last as long as possible.

"If you don't risk anything, Toole, you don't win anything," Peach whispered, in that soft gurgle of his. The gambler surveyed his establishment. Not a soul in it except his staff. Bad business. The funeral had done at least that to him. Not that it made any difference. It was simply female whimsy. He slid a hand to the private counter beneath his layout and extracted a brown glass bottle, rectangular in form, and examined it fondly. Williams' New England Cough Remedy, The Great Family Medicine, Williams and Carleton, Proprietors. He uncorked it and swallowed, feeling the opiate begin its slow work.

"If you use that stuff, they'll bury you for sure," said Toole dourly.

Jubal Peach plugged the cork back in and twisted it, producing a satisfying screech, and lowered the bottle to its shelf. He drew the seven of spades, loser, and ace of hearts, winner, and swept Toole's chip off the layout. Peach heard the rattle of beads sliding on wires.

"There, you see, Sheriff?"

"Who did it and why?"

Jubal paused amiably. "Was it illegal?"

"Not unless there was a body I don't know about in that casket. I may have it dug up."

Peach smiled, reached out, and tapped the table imperiously with delicate white fingers. Sighing, Toole pushed another chip out upon the seven.

"That's better," said Peach. "You can't expect anything for free, Toole, including valuable information. Anaway I'm doing you a favor, giving you a chance to win." He drew the two of spades, loser, and two of clubs, winner.

"Why, I believe I've won," he said, raking in Santiago's chip. That was the house edge in faro, the same card loser and winner. It gave Peach a half a percent house odds if he chose to play a square game. He settled down on his stool and waited benignly, feeling the glory of Williams' Cough Remedy knuckle through him.

"Who did it? I'll get it from Sylvane anyway, but I want it from you."

"It was rather clever, wasn't it?" Peach replied, stroking the dagger-tip of his black mustache. "I'm glad it was first-class. Even a canopy, I'm told. I'd hate to go out fourth-class. And that was some eulogy. I couldn't have done better if I'd written it myself."

It must have cost her a pretty penny, he thought. Five hundred clams at least. And for nothing. Women were silly that way. A show rather than substance. She'd put a dent in his business today, maybe, but she'd lose. He'd see to it. Just a matter of time. If she'd meant to scare him she hadn't succeeded. She wouldn't have the nerve to kill him. The thought of her irked him. Such beauty! Such obvious breeding! Such intelligence. He wasn't sure he liked the intelligence, but he could put up with it. He'd offered her everything, and she'd treated him like a worm, pleading scruples. Intelligence coupled with scruple was like a locomotive driving against brakes. He'd lock her wheels sooner or later.

He rapped a knuckle on the green oilcloth imperiously, and Toole slowly slid a chip, his third, out upon the jack. Then on impulse he "coppered" it, put a copper token on it that said it would lose rather than win.

"Ah, Toole, you've changed your tune. Well, we'll see how coppering works when you buck the tiger."

"I see the burial has affected your business."

"It's only afternoon, Sheriff."

"I suppose it's affected business in your other clubs, too."

"I couldn't say," Peach whispered, pulling a five and a king from the case box. Peach owned six other West End pleasure palaces, ranging from cowboy saloons to fancy joints like this one. In all of them he owned or leased or controlled the gaming layouts, the poker tables, faro tables, monte games, and two roulette layouts, one here in the Buffalo

Hump, the other in the Cottage Saloon. He had all the games in town—except for hers. And that would change soon enough.

"I don't think Tobias got your background just right, Peach," Toole said. "Hattiesburg? Have you ever been near Hattiesburg?"

"I wasn't up there."

"You weren't there, but I'm sure you heard every word of it within minutes."

Peach pulled a ten, loser, and jack, winner, from the case box. He sighed, tongued his damp Eventual to the other corner of his mouth, and pulled in Toole's chip.

"You have bad luck, Sheriff. Or should I call you 'Doctor'?"

"Perhaps someone was sending you a message, Peach."

The sheriff was closing in on it, Peach thought. He'd have it soon enough from that undertaker, but it had been fun to toy with the man. And business was business.

"It could be, Sheriff. I don't know just what the message was, though. You got any ideas?"

He reached under his layout again and clasped the brown square bottle. It felt light. He had twenty-four more, though. They came in boxes of a dozen. He uncorked it and swallowed, feeling the flotation buoy him over Toole's head. "Quite a cough," he said amiably, in his whispery voice.

"You're an addict, Peach. You can control every game of chance in town, but you can't control your body. I think you'd kill to get that stuff if you had to."

"Who says I control every game in town? I'm not a monopolist."

"You'd like to be."

Violently, Peach rapped the oilcloth with his knuckle. The chips rattled. Toole slid his next one out reluctantly, this time on the deuce, right next to the dour case-keeper who kept track of every card with his sliding black beads.

"That's better, Toole." Peach smiled crookedly, letting Toole glimpse his tobacco-browned incisors, and pulled a card from the case box. A trey. The next card was a deuce.

"There, you've bucked the tiger again," he whispered, sliding a chip next to Santiago's. The sheriff plucked it off as if it were a burning brand. The man hated to win. The man wouldn't even accept a few amiable gifts. Peach had pondered that at length in the past. Business would advance a lot easier if Toole would only accept gifts. It wasn't just Toole, either. There was also that crazy justice of the peace, Pericles T. Shaw, uptown. Well, there were always ways and means. And a right time for everything. Like now.

Santiago moved his chip to the queen. Peach slid a nine and a ten from the slot in the case box.

"There. It's on the queen. A good choice, Toole. But queens lose, don't they?"

"You tell me."

The queen would lose. Oh, how she'd lose. Peach pulled a queen loser from the case box and then a seven winner, and swept up Toole's chip.

"I like the queen," Toole said softly, sliding his last chip, the one he'd won, out upon her. "I think she buried you."

Peach laughed softly. "Why do you think that, Sheriff?"

"Who else?"

Peach shrugged. He wanted another slug of Williams' Cough Remedy, but resisted. He was floating too high, and he wished to hover over Toole's head. "Lots and lots of queens in Miles," he whispered.

"Only one, Mr. Peach."

Jubal Peach pulled a queen, loser, and a jack, winner. "The queen lost, Toole. Care to play some more?"

Santiago Toole glared at the empty green board and at Jubal Peach, who sat on his stool chuckling softly.

"I think she won."

"You wouldn't be saying I made a mistake, Sheriff . . . ?"

"I think she won," he said. "No, no more." The slim man in the black frock coat wheeled away. A blinding jolt of sunlight burned Peach's eyes as Toole bulled out the door.

Peach laughed softly and nodded to a stout, short, morose man sitting quietly nearby. Amos Howitzer. "Follow him,

Amos," he whispered. "He'll go see Tobias, and then he'll see her. But I want to be sure of it."

Howitzer nodded and dropped his gray bowler over his center-parted hair.

Peach watched the little man exit and reached for the Williams' again. How could a man go wrong hiring someone named Howitzer, he thought, sucking Cough Remedy.

Santiago found Sylvane Tobias back in his carriage barn, lovingly wiping dust from his new hearse.

"Knew you'd be around," Tobias said. "How was that for a show?"

"He's alive."

"Of course."

"Why?"

"Bought and paid for, five hundred dollars—five hundred!—by Miss Kate."

"A fraud, Tobias."

The cabinetmaker grinned. "A good one, eh? But I hate to see a good walnut coffin go to waste. Do you think it'd be unethical for me to dig it up?" He paused and answered the question himself. "I guess I can't. She paid for it and it's hers."

Santiago parked himself on the nickel-plated running-board. "Tell me about it. From the beginning."

"You sound grumpy, Toole. You're sniffing around like a dog with someone else's bone, looking for something to git mad at. You can't take a joke."

"It's more than a joke, Sylvane. You know that."

"I guess I do." Tobias wiped a black fender delicately and shook his chamois cloth. "Guess I do. She saw me unloading the thing three days ago. They dropped off a flatcar here—you must have seen it."

"I didn't."

"Half the town watched. Some sight! She came over soon enough and bought a funeral, but exactly as she wanted. Five hundred dollars cash money, Santiago. I took her up on it.

She planned everything. Gave me that speech to memorize. Everything.''

"Did she say why?"

"Nope. But it's not hard to figure."

"Is there anything in that casket?"

"Rocks. And a poem in an envelope. Leastwise, she called it a poem. That was some planting, Santiago. Best planting I ever done. Of course, a little cash money helps."

"It could have been a death threat. Maybe you're a part of it."

The cabinetmaker paused. "I took it for fun. How can anyone resist a lady like that? I'd of proposed, pretty near."

Santiago thought of Katherine Dubois, and agreed. What man hadn't thought of marrying her? He had. The thought of it made him feel guilty, and he conjured up Mimi in his mind in expiation.

"Can you tell me anything else, Sylvane?"

The man sighed. "I'd have done it for free. Plum for free."

Toole smiled. "Good planting, Sylvane. Good advertisement, too. What'd this rig cost?"

"Eleven hundred, with black harness and spare pompoms."

"What inspired you? That's money, Sylvane."

"I thought if people knew they could go out in style, they'd croak faster. I hear there's one other, down in Tombstone, Arizona. They croak fast down there, too."

"Good thinking, Sylvane."

Santiago left the man to his dusting and wandered out into the glare. No law broken. No crime. No medical matter. Nothing. But he thought he'd better have a talk with Miss Kate anyway. You give a man a fancy funeral, you're saying something to him.

She owned The Stockman, a large saloon and club on Sixth that cowboys and cattlemen found comfortable. She'd kept it quiet and comfortable, unlike Peach's gaudy places. No one at The Stockman hustled drinks or pressured customers the way they did in Peach's palaces. It boasted a splendid rosewood bar and mirrored backbar, well-lit green baize tables where drovers could play amiable poker, polished brass spittoons conveniently placed, and comfortable stuffed chairs, made for whiling away hours. It had, above all, a fine respectability about it.

The rear third of the long, white, board-and-batt building had been partitioned off into a club room, with a roulette layout, green poker tables, and two faro outfits, the larger one operated most evenings by Miss Kate herself. Originally there'd been no club room, but the town fathers had ordained that no women could loiter in saloons, an ordinance enacted at the behest of Jubal Peach. Miss Kate had simply partitioned off the rear third, making a gaming club of it, and continued on her way. At the rear of her gaming room a small stairway ascended to the second floor, where Miss Kate had her private quarters. No male had ever been up there, according to local legend, except for Dr. Toole, and even he had been accompanied by Miss Kate's maid, Lulu. No breath of scandal ever touched her.

Santiago smiled at that. He'd attended Miss Kate through a severe bout of pneumonia, while Mimi stewed and turned sullen. He'd finally invited Mimi to come along but she'd pouted and refused, preferring to nurse her suspicions and jealousy than to face the truth: that beautiful Miss Kate lay sick abed, half-dead in fact. But the very thought of Santiago up there in Miss Kate's bedroom had been enough to turn Mimi savage.

Santiago walked eastward through late-afternoon traffic, wondering if he'd even see Miss Kate. She usually didn't show up at her faro layout until seven or eight, well after the supper hour. But he thought he'd try. He found himself enjoying the thought of talking with her. Every man in the Territory enjoyed talking with her. Katherine Dubois had a way with men. She knew their first names and listened intently to them. She peered at them through intelligent gray eyes set in a perfect chiseled oval face, with stray wisps of ash-blond hair loose about her, like a halo, and men tumbled like tenpins. Every cowboy coming up the long trail from Texas, every drover out on the ranches, every gandy dancer,

every horn-handed cattleman, every railroad foreman and
superintendent. They came, swooned, played at her crowded
tables gazing wistfully at her while she raked in a fortune—
Santiago guessed that The Stockman did a business equal to
all seven of Peach's palaces—and went off into the night
happy, no matter that they'd plunged every greenback in their
britches.

Which had much to do with the mock funeral, he knew.

If she did consent to see him it would be in the club room,
most likely empty at this late-afternoon hour. And she'd be
wearing the attire that had been her hallmark ever since she'd
arrived two years before, about the time the longhorns began
flowing in from the south. Her ash-blond hair would be tied
into a ponytail with a yellow ribbon, sometimes velvet,
sometimes a floppy bow of silk, but always yellow. She'd
wear a white cotton or silk or linen blouse, elaborately made
with puffed sleeves. At her soft and exquisite throat the white
of the blouse would rise to frame her sublime face and be
caught there by a black velvet choker with an ivory cameo
on it. She had several cameos, with various figures scrimshawed into them, including one with the figure of a pineapple, which had always intrigued Santiago.

With this ensemble she wore long dark skirts, often of fine
wool, clasped at her slender waist with a delicate belt. Somehow she knew the way to burrow into men's souls and hearts,
or rather into their fantasies. They came each night, every
night, glancing at her, drinking her, devouring her. She met
their gazes levelly, her gray eyes intent and inviting, a small
sweet smile on tender lips. And as if drawn by some powerful
magnet, they settled at her table and played. And if hers was
filled—which it usually was—they settled at the next closest
one and paid little attention to their wagers and a lot of attention to her.

She'd always dealt amiably with trouble-makers and blowhards. Men came and demanded her for wife or mistress.
Blowhards offered fortunes in exchange for one night with
her. Jealous cowboys threatened duels with each other over
her. Once a railroad magnate tried to kidnap her. Most of

these brief alarms had been met easily by her own staff, especially an aged, gray old gentleman half bent over with rheumatism, who seemed a most unlikely source of menace to anyone unaccustomed to his fists, the bore of his revolver, or the massive power in his biceps.

Santiago sighed. He loved her as much as every other male did, and wondered at it. Miss Kate was twenty-six. And as silent as a tintype about her past. He'd tried, while attending her illness, to find out about her, but she'd peered up at him, flushed and feverish from her blankets, and said nothing. But Santiago knew what lay behind much of her magic. She'd been born a patrician. Where and when he wasn't sure. He couldn't fathom American accents because he was Irish, but he suspected she'd been born on the East Coast somewhere.

He turned in to The Stockman, enjoying its quiet, amiable solidity, and made his way past the empty bar into the gaming room, which lay silent in the amber light of a single lamp. But there at the far end stood heavy, black-skirted Lulu, with her white hair in a tight bun.

She beckoned him toward the sacrosanct stairwell. "Come this way, Sheriff Toole. She's expecting you."

Chapter 3

Katherine Dubois knew exactly the effect she had on men. She watched Dr. Toole's brown eyes go soft and yearning when he stepped into her sunny parlor, watched his gaze embrace her face and figure and her whimsical smile.

"Dr. Toole," she said softly, holding out a long angular hand. He grasped it.

She preferred to call him doctor. The sheriff part puzzled her. As doctor she knew him and as sheriff she did not, even though his frequent stops at The Stockman were sheriff's duties. Doctors she understood. Indeed, she'd grilled Santiago closely about his practices, his training, his approach to illness, before consenting to be his patient. Toole's training had been splendid—even a student of Lister in Scotland!

His social graces were entirely acceptable, too. She'd spotted it at once, the demeanor of a born aristocrat. In fact she saw qualities in him that nicely pinpointed just who and what he was—traits she knew had eluded the rustics of Miles City.

He pressed her hand, not shaking it, and smiled.

"Have a seat, Doctor," she said softly, motioning him toward a settee. "I have tea."

"Believe I will, Miss Dubois," he said smiling as she poured.

"Did you like the show? I put some thought into it. What a splendid carriage Mr. Tobias has brought us!"

He evaded the question. "I see you're wearing the ivory

cameo with the pineapple engraved in it. I'm curious about
it.''

"It's a family heirloom."

"Yes, but what does it signify?"

"A pineapple is a pineapple, Dr. Toole. A pity we can't
get them here."

It signified family wealth, from pineapples especially but
also from molasses, rum, and slaves, but she wouldn't tell
him that. She'd received it as a gift, and the wealthy family
wasn't her own.

"You're mysterious," he said. "Which is what you wish
to be."

She smiled and brushed a wisp of hair off her brow. Actually, a studied gesture. She'd been born beautiful, and bred
beautiful, but some of it she'd cultivated.

"I'm my own person, that's all."

He sipped. "All right then," he muttered.

"It was a warning, of course. You know that."

He nodded.

"It cost five hundred. I sometimes gross that in a week."

"Twice what medicine yields me in a year."

"Jubal will consider it foolishness, female whimsy, and
proceed."

"That's what I want you to tell me about."

"My funeral parade implies murder. That's what you've
come to see me about."

"Well?"

"That was my message. I'll kill him."

That startled Santiago faintly. "Self-defense?"

"Oh no, Dr. Toole. Premeditated, planned and executed
as a business strategy."

Toole looked amazed. She enjoyed that. The angel of Miles
City had other facets. She'd discovered her other facets as a
girl and had shown them off ever since.

"And what is Jubal Peach's business strategy?"

"Well, let's see. He's proposed partnership, as well as
marriage, as well as ah, a liaison. He's lowered prices of bar
drinks, offered prizes, hired steerers to hustle trade toward

his places. He's offered to buy me out, lease tables, hire me
for whatever I wish to charge him. He's attempted to destroy
my bar supplies—sent people in to poke holes in kegs, break
bottles. He's hired Texas cowboys to smash up the place and
burn it. He's sent toughs and uglies in to intimidate my customers, make scenes, spill drinks, bully my help. He's started
rumors that I cheat, my tables are crooked, my liquor is
diluted. He's tried to bribe teamsters and railroad men who
make deliveries to me. He has, ah, publicly suggested that I
. . . prefer the company of women. He's twice set fire to the
rear of my building. He's slipped marked decks into play at
my poker tables, and then caused someone to complain.
More recently, he's threatened my health—and beauty. Oh
yes, he pushed through that ordinance forbidding women in
saloons—which he ignores himself. And he's been working
on getting the town to employ a city marshal, one he can
control, as long as he can't control you. He's offered to buy
me out entirely. Most recently, he's let it be known that if I
don't leave town standing up, I'll go feet-first. And ah, yes.
A delicate matter, Dr. Toole. He gave me a week to get out
or sell out or I'd be . . . violated.''

Toole settled his Haviland cup back into its saucer, plainly
startled. ''Why?''

''I gross more than all seven of his places put together.''

''I thought as much. Why haven't you told me? Some of
these things are plainly illegal. I have a nice new stone jail.
I knew about one or two fires and one or two disorders, but
not the rest.''

She smiled. ''I take care of myself.''

''So you do. Now, Miss Dubois, how do you intend to
deal with that renegade?''

''A woman never reveals her secrets, Dr. Toole.''

''You're far from your home, lass, and the gentlefolk you
enjoyed in times gone by.''

That surprised her. She said nothing.

''We're fencing, Miss Dubois. From the time we met,
from the time you started your business here, we've fenced.
There's a wall around you, a secrecy you maintain, a certain

mystery you use to entice customers. But you have no friends. I thought perhaps when you had pneumonia and we talked a little about medicine you might lower the veil, but you didn't.''

Fencing . . . Yes, she thought, always fencing. It was safest and revealed the least. ''You don't know me,'' she said softly.

''I know you're in trouble, Miss Dubois. Actually, your name isn't Dubois, is it?''

She stared woodenly at him with unblinking gray eyes.

''A mock funeral is a type of death threat,'' he said softly. ''I should hate to have to arrest you for anything like that. A death threat is, by its very nature, the most extreme gesture you can make, you know. It instantly carries this matter beyond buying and selling and commerce. Doesn't it?''

She nodded slowly.

''I think it'd be best for you to pull back from that sort of thing. I'm here, my office exists, to protect you. And I'll do it. But I can scarcely do my job if you keep secrets from me.''

''It's you who are in danger, Dr. Toole, not I. You're all that prevents Jubal Peach from having his way. And I think before he does anything to me he'll do something to you.''

Santiago Toole nodded. ''Probably true. But you still evade a thing as simple and comfortable as friendship.''

''There can be no simple friendship between a vigorous male and a . . . beautiful woman, doctor.''

He grinned. ''Something to that.''

He'd touched her, but she hated to admit it. She avoided friendships, especially with men, though if she were to choose a friend here she'd choose Toole. But the other things, the passions of the body, would surely intrude. No. No friends. She'd set her life toward adventure, not domestic slavery. She could have been the domestic cow of any of fifty millionaires, supplying docile love and milk to assorted decent, bright children, going the endless round of teas, traveling, yachting, and all the rest. . . . No. She liked this, including the menace of it. Not a woman in a million in this year of 1882 had this.

"I'll remain a mystery. It's for my own protection."

"How'd you learn the games?"

"I was born with them in my head." She laughed easily.

She'd hung around rich men's poker games, games in which mansions and businesses traded hands, watching silently, for if she opened her mouth they'd shoo her off. She'd watched and learned, and now she knew how to wager better than any player she'd studied, even before she played out her first hand.

"You're still fencing. It saddens me somehow, Miss Katherine."

"Perhaps I'm thinking of Mimi, Doctor."

Toole stiffened slightly and then steadied his gaze upon her. He smiled slowly. "A good union is built on friendship, Miss Katherine. Mimi's my best friend."

A good answer, she thought. He could fence, too. She rose. She always controlled social situations, inviting and dismissing as she chose. He hadn't gotten what he wanted, but she'd given him what she intended. She would remain a mystery to Dr. Toole, but Jubal Peach would be no mystery.

He stood. "I'll keep a closer eye on The Stockman."

"You're always welcome."

"Maybe not."

He nodded and found his way out of the parlor and down the carpeted stairs, his footsteps almost silent on the plush nap of the stair-runner.

Katherine had a hunch what Jubal Peach would try next, and thought to prepare for it. She enjoyed that. Peach would be no match for her. She had twice his intelligence, but that wasn't it. She had the imagination and the courage to make use of it. What was the wild American West for, anyway, if not to let a woman lasso clouds, ride broncs, rule empires, and laugh at the gods?

Jubal Peach arrived about ten o'clock, as she had expected, along with that ugly of his, Amos Howitzer. The name tickled her. Kate's own retainers were her maid Lulu and bent old Boris Voroshlikov. Of course Boris had taught martial arts in Tobin's Gymnasium on Thirty-fourth Street in New York City, and he'd taught Lulu the uses of the sap, the stiletto, and the derringer, which she concealed on her ample person.

As usual, both the saloon up front and the gaming club at the rear of The Stockman were jammed. Customers got a generous drink of Old Quaker or Virginia Club up front, for a reasonable price, and a square game in the club at the rear. Miss Kate always wore her white blouse and black velvet choker and cameo, summer and winter. Her dealers always wore white shirts, and never a frock coat. Nothing lay concealed up any sleeve in The Stockman. But that was only the lesser part of it. They came night after night to gaze at her, to crowd her faro layout, make bets scarcely caring about what they bet, just for the reward of her smile, her notice, her direct, frank gaze from intelligent gray eyes. She gave new meaning to the old adage, " 'Tis better to have loved and lost than never loved at all."

The atmosphere changed fast as Jubal Peach entered the saloon. She felt it at once, even back in her club room. A hush descended. The man who'd been buried that very afternoon, for whatever reason, joke or threat, now sauntered lazily past the bar and its silent patrons, his shrewd gaze absorbing everything, the rosewood bar, mirrors, crystal chandelier, generous drinks, the bent old gentleman who seemed to function as major domo. He trailed silence behind him. Customers were plainly curious. Had Jubal Peach taken his funeral for a grand joke?

Peach shifted his Hilt's Best from one side of his sticky lips to the other and puffed, leaving a fine trail of cigar smoke behind him. Miss Kate saw him fill the club room door. He could do that—fill a whole door frame—even though he was neither tall nor blocky nor fat. He filled it with his sheer presence, and a faintly menacing aura that was enhanced by the blocky shadow that trailed in his wake like a dinghy tied to a steamboat.

Miss Kate continued to play, lazily, drawing losers and winners from the case box and announcing them in her soft, throaty voice. But she was losing her players as an autumn willow loses leaves.

"There, you've won, Jake. You can buy Ellie the ring now," she said to a big, beet-red cowboy whose coppered two had been the correct wager. She slid twelve dollar tokens out onto the green baize of her elegant table.

"You're my girl, Miss Kate." He grinned as he plucked up the chips, glanced nervously toward the door, and left.

The next card was the hock, also a two. She pulled the deck from the case box and shuffled adroitly, suddenly alone. Not a player lingered at Miss Kate's table. She smiled, peered about at her other games. At the poker tables the action had stopped, as if suspended by a giant invisible hand. No one had abandoned the poker and monte tables, or her other faro game, or her roulette wheel, but no one played, either. Life froze at the euchre game, the Wheel of Fortune, the black-jack, Hieronymus, and Tarantula; at the paddle wheel and fan-tan.

She nodded faintly to Itzak Ugurplu, her Turk saloon man, who wore black livery that set off his amber face. Itzak knew the uses of whips, broadswords, and crossbows.

"Drinks on the house, gentlemen," she said softly, relishing all this. Miss Kate lived for adventure.

Jubal Peach plowed through yielding air to her table and nodded slightly.

"I trust you are well, Jubal?"

He grunted, settling himself on a stool. Amos Howitzer settled beside Peach, blocky as jack pine and redolent of bay rum. Old Boris materialized beside them, hands out-stretched, and it dawned on them to surrender their derbies to the man. Miss Kate discovered a bluish bald spot on Ju-bal's head she'd never noticed before.

She shuffled idly, waiting.

"That was some sendoff, Kate. You did me proud."

"I'm sorry you weren't present. You'd have enjoyed it, Jubal."

"I thought of coming, since you threw the party for me. But that would've ruint it."

"Oh, no. I hoped you'd hear the eulogy. I wrote it and had Mr. Tobias memorize it. Did I get it right?"

"You have a way with words, Kate."

"But was it right? You didn't talk much about yourself while you were alive."

"Perfect, Kate."

"You needed a good eulogy," she said. "That was the least I could do. The facts of your life were less important than the spirit of it. I tried to catch your essence. I hope Tobias got it all right. Now you'll be remembered."

"Nice headboard, too, Kate. Only you shoulda done it in granite instead of walnut. Granite lasts. Anahow, I appreciate the sentiment. King of Miles City."

"1836 to 1882."

He laughed, and coughed up tobacco.

She nodded, and Lulu magically appeared with a clean brass cuspidor engraved with Cupids.

Peach spat. "That thing's got naked nymphs."

Miss Kate smiled.

"Anahow, I come over to buck the tiger."

She'd anticipated it. Break the bank. His last stab at doing it more or less legally.

"The tiger's ready," she replied. Miss Kate always played a square game. And the house had the thinnest edge in a square game. It won only when the loser and winner were identical cards. It could go either way. She could, of course, refuse and shut down her games. Or keep her five-dollar maximums. But she didn't relish that. She relished what was to come, which bit through her boredom like bee-sting.

"When the bank's busted, double or nothing," he said.

She smiled, not agreeing.

"Double or nothing."

"Tigers have fangs, Mr. Peach."

He nodded to Howitzer, who handed him a heavy pigskin sack. He poured its contents onto the table, scores of shining double-eagles, glinting yellow on the green felt.

She smiled, and gazed around her familiar club room. Itzak quietly served drinks, giving them all Wilken Family whiskey whether they wanted it or not. Boris stood blandly in black, looking bent like a hairpin, his old, ice-blue eyes missing nothing. Above her, high on his stool, her lookout, Eddie Duquesne, peered down at them through gold-rimmed spectacles. Eddie made a good lookout but smelled of stale sweat and unwashed smallclothes. Between Eddie's odors, Peach's yellow cigar, and Howitzer's bay rum, Miss Kate suffered, and worried about a headache.

Miss Kate nodded to Lulu, who headed upstairs to the green safe where seven thousand in greenbacks and three thousand in gold rested for the occasional big game. Lulu would bring only a thousand at a time, the greenbacks first.

Boris gently laid a fresh Pharoah deck on the table. She nodded her approval. Let it all be done with a fresh deck. She broke its seal, fanned it out face-up before Peach, and removed the jokers. Then she shuffled methodically, cards zipping and snapping. She set it before Peach, who cut it thin.

She dropped it in the case box and turned over the soda, a two of hearts. Peach grinned, slid a double-eagle out on the two, and coppered it. She slipped the cards out. Six of spades, loser, three of diamonds, winner. Nothing on the first turn. It would be a boring night with only one player, she thought. She summoned Eddie down from his perch to keep cases. She didn't need a lookout with only one player.

Peach's gaze sought hers, and she read a smirk in him. He blew cigar smoke at her, and she smiled. It beats children and tea in Newport, she thought.

Slowly, the other games resumed. She heard the whirl of the roulette wheel and the rattle of the ivory ball bouncing its way into a pocket. She heard chips clack. She heard the slap of cards. But she didn't hear a human voice, for all the play in her club room proceeded silently. Men played, but their attention was locked on her game.

For an hour it teetered back and forth, a little each way, while Peach puffed and Amos Howitzer stared sullenly at the flared sleeves of her white blouse. Automatically, Itzak Ur-guplu slid fresh glasses of Wilken Family with real lake ice before the players. The Stockman lay peculiarly quiet through the young night, bemused. The stakes weren't particularly high so far and Peach played cautiously, testing his luck. Miss Kate sipped iced tea and wondered what she'd do if she lost. She scarcely thought about winning, and her mind had drifted elsewhere.

Then, around midnight, things changed. Jubal Peach sighed and slid five double-eagles out upon the jack, which hadn't come up after half a deck of play. A hundred dollars now.

She smiled and dealt a seven, loser, and jack of diamonds, winner. From her bank she matched his hundred and he let the two hundred ride, a smirk blossoming around his baggy eyes. That won, too. In a half hour she'd dropped two thousand, and she knew this game had barely begun. Peach whipped his streak hard, upping each bet to three, four, and finally five hundred dollars. Lulu began regular trips up the private stairs for more bank. Kate had never lost like this before and found the experience electric, cutting through the ennui that usually engulfed her. In a way it cut deeper than winning. Jubal Peach didn't gaze soulfully into her gray eyes as all the others did, seeking solace there. If he gazed soulfully at anything it was at the double-eagles and greenbacks heaped before him. She found that a novelty.

Around eleven Sheriff Toole had wandered in and watched silently, following the play. He annoyed her, for reasons she couldn't fathom. He stood quietly in his black frock coat and vest and black britches, that steel star glinting in the yellow of the lamps, standing in the blue saloon haze watching her bank dwindle and Jubal Peach's pile grow. She wished the law would leave. Nothing here was illegal or immoral, even though Toole's flinty glare made it seem that way.

"It's a hemorrhage, Dr. Toole. Have you medicine for that?" she asked sweetly, but he didn't see the humor in it.

Chapter 4

Katherine Dubois had played in long games before, usually poker, but this topped them all. How eerie The Stockman looked in dawn light, all gray and yellow, she thought. The place had long since emptied, except for herself, Boris, Lulu, Peach, and Howitzer. She'd excused her case-keeper and kept cases herself. It was something to do. After the barmen and customers had drifted out at last, her swamper mopped silently into the small hours, and then he left, too. Her body cried and sagged but she ignored it. She wondered how old bent Boris could stand it, sitting patiently at the next table. And faithful Lulu, who frequently had run up the stairs to her safe for another thousand . . . and had brought her the last thousand—the last of the bank.

Peach had far more cash on hand; she knew that. She did a large gaming business but her games were square and her profits smaller than his. He'd weathered a long, long losing streak that would have sunk ordinary mortals, or at least intimidated them, and then his luck had turned. All night he'd played large bets, running two hundred and up, while sucking from his brown bottle of Williams' New England Cough Remedy, his pupils wide and open, revealing his mocking naked soul. Boris refilled the lamps twice and fed the stove hourly, but still they played. Never had life been as intense as this.

Her shoulders and back ached; her arms throbbed from the constant dealing, sliding the cards out of the case box, loser, winner, soda and hock, twenty-five turns between shuffles. He read her well and sensed victory, protected from his own weariness and pain by the juices he swallowed regularly, sometimes mixed with Wilken Family to make some awful concoction.

He won another, two hundred on a coppered eight. "Anaway, you're sinking," he said. "You don't bury Jubal without paying."

She nodded slightly and turned loser and winner.

"I got so I enjoyed it, burying my carcass. You got me to thinking. Maybe I'll bury myself once a year. Town enjoyed it. Parade, speech, band. Best publicity I ever had. Nobody forgets Jubal Peach."

She nodded. Loser, winner.

"Anaway, you're sinking. Unless you want to deal."

She said nothing. No deals.

He won again, this time with a big four-hundred bet, and her remaining bank shrunk starkly. He gazed at her from wide, opiated eyes, a faint smile building. Usually when the bank ran this low Miss Kate nodded to Lulu. But this time she didn't nod.

She kept her bank on a shelf behind her. He studied it, shifting a gummy Cub around his puffy lips, and smiled. Then he studied the cases and slid twenty-five double-eagles out upon the jack. No jack had been played. He settled back and sighed happily. She turned the cards: loser a jack; winner a jack. Unsmiling, she raked in the gold and kept cases. He frowned.

"That about paid for my funeral," he said. "Heard it cost you five hundred."

She sipped water, feeling herself sag and sleep seduce her. She doubted she could last much longer. She could turn it over to Boris, of course. But she wouldn't. This was her fight. Howitzer looked woozy, and more asleep than awake. Lulu slumped in a chair.

"You come work for me and I'll go home. In fact I'll give you back what I've won. I own the game and The Stockman; you get a quarter for running it and playing every night, just like now."

She shook her head.

"Anaway, it's a fair offer, Kate."

She dealt, a six and nine. No one won.

"How about double or nothing? We'll each draw a card. You win, you get my winnings back. I win, I get twice, which means this joint and your games."

She shook her head wearily.

"Can't you talk? Too tired? Too frail?"

"I don't make desperation bets."

He pulled the squeaking cork from his brown bottle and lifted it, sucking greedily. A bit of the murky fluid dribbled onto his chin. He corked it up. "Anaway, I'm holding up," he said softly. "Want some?"

She shook her head and dealt. Two, loser, king, winner. His king bet won three hundred. She eased the double-eagles across to him and adjusted the cases. The next card was the hock. She pulled out the deck and shuffled, letting him cut. The soda was the four of clubs.

"Last deal," he said, smiling. He bet the seven.

No one won. The late-summer sun crept up, casting blinding beams through the windows of The Stockman. Outside, people stirred.

"It's a new day, Jubal."

For a while the game seesawed. She dealt with leaden hands, by rote, her mind numb. She feared she'd slip into sleep, lose her alertness, allow him to cheat somehow. He sprawled in a chair—they'd abandoned their stools—waiting for it, waiting to see what he would do, sustained by his opium.

"Lulu, I want coffee," she said sharply. But Lulu slept. "Wake her," she snapped at Boris. The old man gently shook Lulu, who peered sourly around and disappeared. Some vast anger gripped Katherine, fueling life back into her aching body. Outside, people peered through the windows and rattled the locked door, but The Stockman remained closed. Word of the great struggle had obviously spread. Her head throbbed and settled into a pulsing migraine.

It was odd. Neither she nor Peach had paused to visit the

necessary rooms. She felt no need. Her body had been mes-
merized by this struggle. She sat, loathing him, hating his
greed, his smirk, his contempt, his threats to her, his seductions, his obsession with having it all, locking up all the
games in Miles City, destroying her if she resisted. Jubal
Peach. A name that sounded like spitting in her mind, a
name that reminded her of worms and slugs and cock-
roaches.

"Anaway," he said, picking up some long-abandoned
thread of thought, "your little funeral wasn't heeded. Know
what I mean? I never looked down the bore of a cannon.
When you make a statement you got to make me believe it."

She feared that. She slid her hand to a small shelf below
the board and clasped her over-and-under derringer. She
whipped it up and pointed it steadily at Peach's heart. He
blinked, glanced nervously at the dozing Howitzer, and
swallowed hard, his lips flapping but no words coming out.
She held it on him, let him peer into the two lethal bores, let
him sweat and ooze opium from his oily pores. "Now do
you believe it?" she asked softly.

It took him a minute to respond. He glanced at Howitzer.
Then he smiled. "You wouldn't."

She brought the derringer up again and cocked it, the click
loud in the shadowed dawn.

He sat frozen. "I believe you." She put the little weapon
back. He pushed gold pieces out on the board.

Then he won three hundred on the king, and four hundred
on the ace, and her bank came up two hundred shy. Done.

"You've broken my bank."

He smirked. "You owe me two hundred. Now."

"You may have that faro layout. It's worth more."

"No. Cash."

Boris had come awake and glared sharply. She nodded
and he headed out into the bar. Lulu brought steaming coffee. It had taken her time to build a fire and heat water.

Boris handed her the bar receipts from the previous night.
They came to ninety-three dollars.

"Here."

Peach counted and smirked. "You owe me a hundred and seven. Now." He glared at Amos Howitzer, who'd come full awake.

"I'll have it to you before noon."

"Double or nothing. I win, I get the place. You win, you get your bank back."

"No."

"Then pay." He gazed at her with dark amusement. "You can pay me upstairs, Virgin Kate."

"Get out."

Old Boris erupted to life. "Out," he said. "You've insulted a lady."

"Gamblers aren't ladies. That's a fancy pose for the cowboys."

She dashed her hot coffee over him. Amos Howitzer landed on her, twisting her arm violently. Old Boris, using some Russian maneuver she'd never seen, sent Howitzer somersaulting through space. Howitzer landed against a poker table, gashing his head. When he collected himself he peered into the bore of Boris's small revolver. Howitzer looked amazed, and blood ran down his nose.

"Out," said Boris.

"You owe me," said Peach.

"You'll get it," she said, the last of her energy leaking away.

"I'll attack the place."

"Try it."

Boris prodded them toward the front door, unlocked it, and shoved them out. He locked it again.

"We'll have to watch for fires again," he said.

She slumped at her table, her mind drifting. Broke. A fascinating experience, but not new to her. And yet not broke. She couldn't run table games without a bank, but she had a bar, which a city ordinance prevented her from entering. She owed on the building and couldn't make payments without the games. Odd, being broke. She probably could scrape up the hundred and seven from cash in her purses upstairs. There'd be money in the bar accounts too. An interesting proposition, she thought. No way to pay her help. Or buy supplies, especially whiskey. She thought of the things she could do to recoup, and fast. But she wouldn't do them. She would not sell her beauty. That was a contract she'd made with herself when she'd abandoned her life in the East. Honor in all things. She'd adventure in ways women never adventured, and she'd do it honorably or not at all. She wasn't religious, but she admired certain of the moral precepts her mother had drilled into her. They had served her well, enabling her to enjoy a life that few women experienced without turning into the sort of person who'd live and die weeping into her pillow.

"Go to bed," she said to her solemn entourage. "We'll open the bar tonight. I believe I have enough loose cash upstairs to pay the last hundred and seven."

She dragged herself up the stairs, not knowing what the future would bring but curious about Fate.

Jubal Peach blinked at the early sun, finding it hostile and alien. Behind him old Voroshlikov snapped the lock of The Stockman thunderously, like a boot to the butt. Peach's soft pigskin satchel lay heavy in his hand, filled with ten thousand dollars of gold and greenbacks. The new wealth didn't matter to him. What set him to gloating was that he'd busted her. Behind that echoing door lay ruin. Near ruin, anyway. He'd polish her off in a day or two.

He loped toward the Buffalo Hump, his eyes watering in the brightness, faster than Howitzer could keep up. He seethed at the short-legged hunk of beef trailing him. Kate Dubois had pulled a derringer on him, almost murdered him on the spot, and Howitzer had dozed through it. He boiled at the remembrance of it: those black bores, her steel-gray eyes, his helplessness—and Amos Howitzer, stupid with sleep.

"You almost got me killed," he snarled.

Howitzer said nothing.

"She meant to do it—saw it in her eyes. And there you snoozed."

"Want me to fix her?" Howitzer asked, by way of contrition.

"Yes."

"Got any preferences?"

"Make it hurt. And don't you ever let me down again."

"I'll make her remember, before she forgets."

"Plan it, Howitzer. Don't be obvious. I don't want Toole landing on me."

Howitzer was a man without subtlety, Peach thought. You could point him at a target and pull the lanyard, and there'd be a crater where there wasn't one.

"Tonight. I'm tired of waiting. Get some sleep today. Then get up tonight and do it."

They reached the Buffalo Hump and Peach unlocked the grimy door. The place looked odd, shabby in the morning light, its whitewash grimy, its shiplap splintered. The ornate red letters up on the false front, the ones saying BUFFALO HUMP CELEBRITY HALL, looked faded. He'd never noticed that.

The dark saloon smelled rank in the dawn air, redolent of stale beer and last night's vomit. They trudged past tables with chairs perched on them, where the swamper had left them, and then separated, Peach to his dark office and Amos Howitzer to the apartment lean-to at the rear of the long, thin building. Peach wanted his security on hand at all times, and had had quarters tacked onto the building.

He lit a kerosene lamp in his office and dialed the combination for his small gray safe, one made of laminated steel plate by Hooper and Walheimer of Milwaukee. Seven left, thirty-eight right, four left, and twenty right. The door swung open silently and Jubal Peach unloaded his original stake and the winnings, stacking the gold neatly and squaring the bills. Later he'd count the bills into thousand-dollar packets and tape them. He swung the door shut, hearing the satisfactory clicking as the tumblers fell back into place.

Then he settled into his quilted black-leather Morris chair and pulled out his Williams' Cough Remedy. He'd have a small victory celebration before going home, a double dose of paradise.

He wasn't much pleased by his great victory. She still had her saloon. At least until Howitzer got done with her. How close he'd come! He'd broken her bank and then offered double or nothing on the turn of a card. She had had an exactly even chance to recover her bank. But she refused! From Jubal's standpoint, that would have been the perfect wager. If he'd lost, he merely would have returned what he'd won and not have been out a cent. He simply would have tried to break her bank again. If he'd won, he would have had her place, her furnishings, her liquor, and maybe her, if he pressured her enough. And that would have meant he owned the whole tenderloin in Miles City, undisputed. He could have raised drink prices, braced the decks, owned the sheriff, diluted the booze, all without competition, except from a couple of soldier dives he didn't bother with. In fact, he'd have found it convenient to let a few hellholes stay independent. If hard things needed doing, such as busting someone's kneecaps or worse, it would pay not to have it happen in his own saloons.

But she'd refused an even bet! Refused to get her bank back! She would keep on serving her generous, low-priced booze, pour bonded whiskey, and undercut him badly. At least until Howitzer did something about it. Coldly, he pondered her assets. She had the building. She had a stock of good booze. She had a large and loyal patronage. She had the goodwill of the sheriff and the JP. And . . . she had beauty and breeding of a sort that set men to yearning and gazing and hungering and drawing around her just to experience her presence. That was her real asset, he thought, her splendid face and form. She added poise and education and kindness to it, and what man could resist?

He sighed. He'd tried everything. He'd tried arson and had considered trying again, until he realized that a spreading fire might torch the whole town, his own saloons included. It came down to Miss Kate. It always came down to Miss Kate. He'd proposed every sort of partnership, alliance, agreement, and she'd laughed at him. He'd tried to drive her out of Miles, shut her down with town ordinances, and still she flourished. He could destroy her place, and still she'd be there. As long as she could bewitch helpless, lovestruck men, she'd have the edge over him. He thought about that and its implications and the beginnings of a plan took hold in him.

He guzzled another jolt of Williams' New England Cough Remedy. It always took a few minutes to work. The stuff owned him, but it didn't matter. He'd never imagined there could be such an easy means to get through life painlessly. He turned out the lamp, locked the front door, and stepped into the morning. The glaring sun hurt his eyes, and he pulled his green celluloid spectacles from his frock coat to protect his vision.

Not until he entered his parlor, with its tight-drawn velvet drapes, did his eyes stop hurting. The woman sat there, almost invisible. He tucked his green celluloid spectacles into his breast pocket and stared. She seemed to be in her usual anguish, her left hand clamped over the wrist of her right to stop the tremors.

"I busted her. Broke her bank," he said affably.

"I need it. Get some for me," she whispered. He spotted wetness on her cheeks.

"I'm King of Miles City. She wrote it right on my marker."

"Please . . . Please, Mr. Peach."

"A great day. I've been working for this. Few odds and ends still. Best day in years."

"You were gone so long. . . . I almost came," she whispered, trembling.

That would have been disgusting, he thought. Having the woman walk into The Stockman in the middle of the big game. "I'd have thrown you out."

"I need it. You were away so long, and I ran out."

"Fix me a meal. Breakfast."

"I can't."

Of course she couldn't. The tremors convulsed her so violently she couldn't break an egg or lift a cast-iron spider. He pulled the brown bottle from his frock coat, uncorked it, and swilled slowly.

"Give me," she begged, more tears forming.

"Breakfast. We have to celebrate. I'm ten thousand dollars richer this morning."

"I . . . can't. There's nothing here."

He felt the Cough Remedy suffuse his body, subduing his irritation at her. She'd started to annoy him.

"You should take care of me better. I provide for you. I give you . . . what you need."

"Don't do this anymore," she whispered. "You always do this."

He laughed. "Why don't you quit?"

She wept while her body convulsed, out of control.

"You're ruining my day. Here it is, a red-letter day. A banner day. I am King of Miles City. And there you are, whining and sobbing. You're disgusting. You don't even have the courage to—"

"Jubal, My God, Jubal."

"I am Mr. Peach. Here." He pulled the brown bottle from his frock coat again and held it. She stood, trembling, and lurched for it. He danced the bottle away. She lurched again, and he laughed. She fell on the rose-patterned Brussels carpet, clutching herself, silent now.

"You belong to me," he said softly. "You should treat me better."

He squatted beside her and uncorked the rectangular bottle. Her hands were too unsteady to lift it, so he helped her. She drained the rest of it, tablespoons of it.

In a few minutes the tremors slowed and stopped, and she peered up at him through the brown shadow of the room.

"What do you want to eat?"

"Nothing. I'm not hungry. I'm going to bed."

"Leave me some first!"

"All right. Otherwise you'll pester me."

She followed him to his darkened bedroom. He unlocked

the armoire and gazed benignly on his hoard, two dozen bottles in white cartons plus a single bottle more, and handed her the single bottle, smiling.

Chapter 5

Mimi awakened him from an afternoon siesta.

"You've got a patient. There's a woman waiting."

Santiago yawned, noting the motes illumined by bright sun. "Who?" he asked.

"I think it is Mrs. Peach. I've seen her only once."

Mrs. Peach. Santiago yawned again, rubbing his eyes, and clambered off the bed. Mrs. Peach. He'd never treated her before. He tried to conjure her up in his mind, but could only recollect a gaunt, faceless blonde lurking invisibly in the shadows of the Peach brick pile on Palmer Street. A shadow-woman.

He found her sitting in the armchair and realized he'd never viewed her in sunlight before. She was short and gaunt, with an unhealthy pallor and hollowness around her eyes. But she wore a costly brown silk dress, and a fancy ruffled brown hat lay pinned into her dull blond hair.

"Mrs. Peach? What may I do for you?"

She surveyed him from hazel eyes, her gaze lingering on his sleepy face.

"I was having a siesta. I was up late last night, in fact, watching Mr. Peach at Miss Kate's table. Quite a game."

She grimaced. "It ended in the morning," she said dully. "That's when he came home."

"What may I do for you?"

"I'm not Mrs. Peach, I'm Anna Waldevsky. Sometimes I'm presented as Mrs. Peach."

"Well, that's fine. You've come for something?"

43

"I don't know what I've come for."

"Well, perhaps I can take a history, and then we'll see what to do. How old are you, Miss Waldevsky?"

"I'm Anna. Twenty-nine."

That shocked him. She looked fifty. Indeed, she looked not so much physically ill, though that was a part of it, as melancholic, despondent.

"Where do you hurt?"

"I don't know."

"Would you like just to talk a bit?"

"I guess."

"Does Mr. Peach know you're here?"

"No. He's asleep in his room. He'll go to the club later."

Santiago sensed that the conversation was leading nowhere, and his efforts to help her talk weren't availing, so he settled back in his desk chair and sipped Arbuckle's silently.

At first she seemed flustered by his silence. He saw words form on her lips and then vanish, saw her gaze dully at his paraphernalia, his microscope, his yellowed skeleton, his gray books and green tins of *materia medica*. Her gaze settled at last on an ivory skull.

"I saw the funeral," she whispered. "I heard the music and went. I was in the crowd, so you didn't see me. I thought Jubal was dead. I didn't know he was still in the Buffalo Hump."

This turn of conversation didn't surprise Santiago. He nodded patiently, yawning again, wanting more sleep. She fiddled with her hands and the brown silk of her dress.

"I thought he was in the casket."

Awareness leapt through Santiago. "You thought Jubal was really being buried? And no one had told you he died? And you were, ah, his widow?"

She smiled wanly. "I was shocked. I couldn't understand it—Jubal being buried. And I didn't know. *No one told me*."

"You must have felt . . . terrible. All alone. No one in Miles City knows you, Mrs.—Anna."

"Yes, alone. But I didn't feel anything, Except maybe good."

"Good?"

She nodded grimly. "Wouldn't you feel good if Jubal Peach disappeared? He doesn't care about me. No one cares. That's why they buried him without telling me. No one cares."

"So you were there, thinking he'd died."

"Yes, I was there. I didn't know. He came home later and I fainted at the sight of him. I thought he was a ghost! I shook so badly I couldn't even drink the syrup. He told me it was just Miss Kate's little joke. But it wasn't a joke."

"No, not a joke. A reply to Jubal. A threat. Isn't that the case?"

"Jubal was in a rage and drank a lot of Williams' Cough Remedy—that's just opium, you know. I do it, too. That's why I look so tired."

Santiago said nothing, noting the ravaged flesh and face and understanding the causes.

"He made me, at first. Made me drink it until I needed it, and then he had me hooked, a prisoner forever."

"You'd thought of leaving?"

She nodded. "Who wouldn't?"

"And now you can't?"

"Not and live respectably. I was just a girl—I met him when I was nineteen, in Kansas City. He ran games there and seemed so . . . so dashing. My parents disapproved but I had to have my way."

"You want to break the addiction; you came to me for help?"

"No. I don't want to break it. It's the only thing I want. I don't want anything else. When Jubal died . . . when I thought he'd died . . . I felt wild. I'm all alone in the world. Where would I get it? The bottles?"

Santiago sat, puzzled. He had no inkling of why she'd come, unless just to talk with a physician.

"When I saw Jubal's casket being lowered into that hole, I thought about death. I'd never thought about death before. But I thought about it. No one really cared about him. I could see it in the faces. They were curious, that's all. That man,

Sylvane Tobias, didn't even sound sincere. But there was
Jubal down there, his life gone out of him forever, all done.
And they didn't care.''

"You cared, though. You must have cared."

Tears formed in her hollow eyes. "I did, in a way. But all
mixed up. He'd cared for me—for the first year or so. Once
he was tender and dashing and a good—and a husband, until
he made me his slave and owned me and made me beg for
the bottles.''

She dug into her reticule and found the familiar brown
square bottle. With a squeal she ripped off the cork and guzzled Cough Remedy, then carefully corked it again.

"You see, I'm a slave."

"There's emancipation, but it's not easy."

"There's death," she retorted. "I thought about death for
the first time up there. When you're young you hardly ever
think of it. It happens to someone else. But I thought about
death. About me, coming to the end. Of dying all alone,
because no one knows me. I lack for friends, you know.
Who'd be a friend of the woman of Jubal Peach?''

"I would," said Mimi softly from the door.

Her presence startled them both. She pressed a cup of tea
on Anna, who refused it. Santiago cocked an eye at Mimi.
She was a famous eavesdropper, with a penchant for barging
in about the time his male patients were dropping their
britches. She smiled at him.

"It's too late," said Anna. "Up there at the cemetery I
knew my turn would come. And I'd be alone. I've been alone
ever since I . . . ran off with Jubal. I've been all alone."

"Well now you're not," Santiago said.

She ignored him. "Alone. When my times comes, I'll be
alone. I won't have any children. I won't have any brothers
or sisters or grandchildren or anyone else to hold my hand
and help me when I'm sinking. I won't have a soul around
me except Williams' Cough Remedy, and I'll sink away all
alone and never come back. And if there's a God, he'll not
bother with me. I'll be alone there, too. You don't know
what alone is until you've lived around Jubal Peach and drunk

cough syrup. He lives alone. I live alone. He never says anything kind. He just orders me and expects me to tend house. All alone. I've gone for weeks without saying a word to another mortal. I'm dead. I should have been in that box. Let me tell you, that funeral or whatever it was—joke—started me going.''

Santiago scarcely knew how to help a human being in such a state. Rebuild her health? He'd have to wean her from opiates and repair her spirit, too. ''Do you eat well? Do you have variety in your menu? Vegetables and meats, grains and fruits?''

She laughed dourly. ''He eats at his clubs. I just catch what's around.''

''You could leave, you know.''

She flared at him, as if he'd said something stupid. ''With what? Who'd buy my bottles? If I need . . . bottles, could you give them to me?''

At last he understood. ''I can't supply your . . . needs. But if you were desperate I could give you a minimum dose, say, three grains of Dover's Powder.''

''That's all?'' She looked defeated.

''That's all.''

''I'm so lonely. I'm all alone.''

''Perhaps I can find ways to help you, Anna. If you want help. You have to want.''

''I don't want. I don't want!'' she cried. And bolted out the door, while Santiago and Mimi stared.

Old Boris Voroshlikov stood at Santiago's door late that afternoon.

''Miss Dubois desires that you attend her,'' he said.

''Is she unwell?''

''I believe so.''

''I've a patient now, and then I'll be along directly,'' Santiago said.

Miss Kate unwell? Simple exhaustion, probably. That morning, after Mimi had relentlessly awakened him, Santiago had done his morning rounds, finding nothing amiss.

Chang Loon had fed the sole prisoner in the jail, a drunken cowboy. Santiago had taken the old drover to the justice of the peace, Pericles T. Shaw, who interrupted his reading of Heraclitus's *Cosmic Fragments* long enough to fine the man two dollars. After that Santiago had peered into the quiet saloons on the west side of town, only one of them open mornings, and had at last peered into The Stockman, finding it dark. No lamplight issued from the club room at the rear, so the great game must have ended.

He closed the door on Voroshlikov and returned to his patient, Joshua Garrand, a harnessmaker who'd started a Miles City business the year before. Garrand, a burly bachelor, suffered from phthisic, and now gasped for breath. He feared suffocation, and dared not even lie down for fear of expiring. He struggled for air, and wheezed each breath. The veins on his forehead were distended.

"The worst one yet," he gasped. "Seems hours."

"We'll get you past it, Joshua," Santiago said, not very sure about it.

Phthisic, or asthma, was a mysterious disease, and Santiago felt a helplessness in dealing with the man. It seemed to arise from such things as dust in the air, or odors, even perfume. Current medical opinion favored the idea that it was a nervous disorder, triggered by fright, bad news, grief, and things of that nature. Santiago wasn't sure. Most treatments involved chloroform or ether, or narcotics, but Santiago shied away from that. He preferred an antispasmodic and relaxant, made of equal parts of the tinctures of lobelia, capsicum, and skunk cabbage root, taken half a teaspoon at a time every ten or fifteen minutes. Another good one was stramonium leaves, pulverized by hand, plus an ounce of saltpeter. A half teaspoonful on a hot shovel yielded a medicinal smoke that induced therapeutic coughing.

"Try this," he said, folding the lobelia formula for Garrand. On the label he scribbled the dosage, making sure he wrote clearly. He had a careless hand. "You'd best abandon the harnessmaking for the day and stay quiet. If this doesn't work we'll go to some other remedies, eh?"

The suffering harnessmaker nodded, too weary to speak.

"Lie down, lad. Don't be afraid to lie down. If you're in trouble, we'll go to a narcotic."

Santiago watched him lumber out, worried that the bachelor, who lived alone, could not summon help if he needed it. The disease had no cure, only palliatives. Things like that always depressed him.

No more patients. He grabbed his Gladstone, making sure he had powders for whatever ailed Miss Kate, stopped in the bedroom where Mimi was cleaning the chamber pot to kiss her and tell her he was on his way to The Stockman—she glared dourly at him upon learning that—and left. Minutes later that ample ancient maid, Lulu, was escorting Santiago up the darkened staircase and into the quiet apartment above.

He found her staring at the corniced ceiling, the white counterpane pulled high and modest and her face ravaged: eyes dark, bagged, and hollow, flesh gray, and hair greasy and straggled. Was this the beautiful Kate Dubois who celebrated life and joy each night below?

Lulu hovered near, a duenna, a seal of Miss Kate's virtue. Miss Kate didn't smile.

"Boris summoned me," he said.

She nodded. "You have the news, of course."

"I can guess it."

"It was over about half past seven. He broke my bank."

"I'm sorry."

"I've tried to sleep and can't. I'm unwell, too. Perhaps you have powders."

"Unwell?"

"My head. My throat. I'm hot."

He settled himself beside her and took her hand, finding it icy. He slipped a thermometer into her mouth and pulled out his stethoscope.

"I'll need to listen," he said gently.

She nodded, and he pulled back the cover. She wore a thin white nightgown, dampened by her fever so that it clung. He tried to think of anything—of Mimi, of wind and stars and moon, of cadavers and medical texts and gray pickled organs—but he couldn't.

Her young heart sounded fine and her lungs clear. He pulled the thermometer and found fever, but under a hundred. He peered into her throat with his laryngoscope and found it red and inflamed.

"Where does your head hurt?"

"All over. It throbs. My temples mostly."

"You're exhausted."

"You're not telling me anything."

He pulled the coverlet back up. The curve of her breasts under the damp gown had been too much for him.

"I consider all fever dangerous," he said. "We have so little to fight it. But so far, at least, this seems under control. I'd say it's the result of great shock, of great sorrow or fright. Such as one would expect after playing through the night and past dawn, and losing it all."

"Not all. I have the place still."

"Suffering great loss, then."

"I'm not done. I have the saloon. But I'll have to let most of my people go. And I may not be able to keep up with my mortgage."

"That's a headache."

She smiled wanly. "I've thought about it. If I could just be with my customers, the place might still draw trade. But I can't. You'd arrest me. I can't even be in my own saloon during business hours. Peach has serving women and ignores his own law."

True, thought Santiago. Here he was again, medicine and law joining and colliding. Odd how his vocations jostled each other.

"I've failed to enforce that ordinance," he confessed. "I hate it, and no one cares anyway. I should either do it uniformly or . . . see what Pericles Shaw will do about it."

Miss Kate's financial future, he knew, depended on her presence in her saloon. If she was there the cowboys and gandydancers and soldiers would still come, even if her games had been shut down.

"I hope it'll be repealed."

"Maybe that's the best medicine," he said. "Hope cures."

"My head is coming off."

Nervous headache. Not brow ague, or rheumatic or gouty headache. Not uraemic or alcoholic headache. It was nervous or hysterical headache, not uncommon. Relief usually came from anodynes or narcotics, or bromide compounds, given as headache powders.

"I could give you a narcotic anodyne, but I'd rather not. I'd rather you just weather it, Miss Dubois."

"You want to save me from Peach's habits."

"A young woman, vibrant and healthy, ought not to take opiates."

"He did. All night. He didn't even grow weary. He drank that disgusting stuff right from the bottle, and just relaxed happily through the whole game. He never needs sleep."

"It wasn't really a game, was it?"

"He wanted to destroy me."

"They why did you play?"

"A house can't choose customers."

"You usually set limits. Five or ten a turn, I believe."

She nodded. "There are some slight odds for the house. And . . . I suppose I wanted to let it happen. I made up my mind when I started on my own to live to the hilt."

He nodded, staring at the young woman who suddenly looked terribly old. "Living that way, night hours, smoky rooms, alcohol, men with loosened tongues and purposes, Miss Kate, that can drain you of vitality, of the energetic essence. It can lead you to female complaints, the frets and weariness, and neuralgia, such as this."

She smiled. "You sound more like a preacher than my doctor."

He wanted to tell her that saloon living would take the bloom off of her faster than anything he knew of, but he bit it back. It was her life. She'd have pulmonary complaints soon from all the tobacco haze and lamp smoke of her daily life. Even now she coughed violently from time to time. And he'd be forced to watch her helplessly.

"I know what you're thinking," she said. "But there's the other side. I broke out. No woman has ever enjoyed what I enjoy. And I'm respectable, too. I'm a . . . maiden. An old maid. That's the price of this. I made the bargain with myself. No men, in exchange for freedom. Freedom! I'm the only woman in the country who has it! Some don't think I'm very proper, but in my own eyes, and the eyes of those who know me well, I am. I did it. It may shorten my days, but what days!"

Santiago had no answer to that. He wondered how she'd feel in old age, with no children, no grandchildren to hug and love. Would she regret a life spent lavishly on . . . herself?

"I'd like powders," she whispered. "My head's coming off."

Reluctantly, Santiago dug in his Gladstone for the bottle of three-grain doses of Dover's Powder.

"Just this once. I promise."

"I'll take you at your word. And leave a single dose, Miss Dubois."

"I live at the reckless edge," she said. "At the edge is joy and pain. It's better than living in dull safety, now isn't it?"

Chapter 6

The mock funeral had started it in her. At twenty-nine Anna Waldevsky had scarcely thought of death. But that fraud up in the cemetery had unloosed it. She saw herself dying, a helpless addict, alone. She knew herself to be half-dead already, a slave, anxious about the next bottle, whether or not Jubal would give it to her or hold out and make her suffer, perhaps tantalize her as he often did, handing her the bottle only to snatch it back just as her trembling hands grasped it.

She didn't want to die. But when she'd watched that casket slide into its hole, she knew Jubal's fate would soon be her own—unless she did something. Anything! She'd gone to Dr. Toole and he'd suggested escape. As if she could escape! No mortal was as much a prisoner as she! Still, the idea worked in her mind, fevered it. Obsessed, she paced the darkened brick pile Peach called home, wondering what to do. Something! Anything!

Air! Sunlight! Yesterday Dr. Toole had suggested she get out, take air, discover the sun, eat well. Violently she ripped open the heavy drapes, jammed them away from the windows, until eerie chalky light exploded into every corner of the parlor. She stood in the middle of the morning sun, seeing motes. In this place of Peach's she'd never seen a mote of dust. She saw sun on her gray, yellowish flesh and despaired. Where had her youth gone, the peaches-and-cream complexion she'd been so proud of? It'd been eaten away by a bottle, a thousand bottles.

Bottles that owned her. When Toole had suggested she

53

might free herself from the one thing that made life bearable, she'd fled, horrified. She'd never surrender her bottles. Still, each day she died a little more, and life had scarcely begun. She'd become the strangest sort of old maid, unmarried but married. She raced up the stairs and flung apart the drapes in her room, the heavy opaque drapes that veiled her sanctuary in perpetual gloom and hid her own acts from herself.

The light dazed her. It raked the room mercilessly. Light had no pity; light was cruel and brutal, whipping her, lacerating her. How could light do that? She blinked in the glare, her eyes unaccustomed. She threw herself across the unmade bed, blinded by the glare, and pressed her eyes shut, seeing red dots throb past her vision, the sunlight piercing even through her closed eyelids. She hated that light but didn't want to close the drapes again, didn't want the safety of blackness. Tension twisted her, and the bed itself resisted her. Tautly she found her reticule and its precious burden. She clasped the familiar brown glass and pulled the cork and sucked at the bottle he'd given her. A swift sure peace descended, and she lay back quietly in the unaccustomed glare. A quarter of it left. She would need another, soon now. It gnawed at her, her not having enough and Mr. Peach away at the Buffalo Hump. He almost lived there. She'd have to go to him, interrupt, beg in front of them all. Beg him to open the locked door of his armoire. Beg . . . .

An idea formed in the mists of her imagination, but it seemed so obscure she couldn't grasp it at first. The idea loitered on the doorstep of her mind, not entering, not revealing itself, even though she opened her arms to it and begged it to enter. And then she knew.

In Jubal's room lay her salvation, twenty-four fresh bottles. Enough to escape with! Enough for two months if she were careful! And nothing but a flimsy lock between the bottles and her. She could break that door with a crowbar. He had lots of tools below, out in the rear lean-to. But if she took the bottles he'd kill her. She had to leave if she took them. But where? And with what? She lacked money. East. To her family. They'd welcome her; she knew they would.

She'd work in the big mercantile with her brothers. She'd earn enough to buy the bottles and they'd never know. She'd go home, and if they chastened her for running off with Jubal she'd listen humbly.

She needed money. Enough to buy a coach seat on the eastbound and escape, escape. She'd have to hurry, too. Jubal might return from the Buffalo Hump at any moment. That's where he kept his money—in the safe. But not all of it. He kept some here; she knew that.

She stood up shakily, hating the white sunlight but liking it too, and slipped down the stairs and out the back door. She found a crowbar, heavy and black, carried the cold iron back up the quiet stairs, and entered Jubal's room. She couldn't bear the blackness of it, the faint mustiness of it, so she wrenched the massive drapes back and let sunlight blister this place too, turning everything white and merciless.

Then she jabbed the bar into the crack of the armoire door and yanked. Wood splintered but the lock held. She yanked savagely, and this time the polished oak shattered and the door slammed open. There they were, two white boxes, a dozen a box, glowing dimly. And there lay a small brown canvas pouch, stuffed with something. She pulled the boxes out and opened them, hearing glass clink on glass. Bottle after bottle. Some vast anxiety slid out of her then, the unnamed terror of not having a bottle when she needed one. She unbuckled the small pouch and found it stuffed with small bills, ones, twos, fives, tens. In all, many hundreds of dollars. Enough. She'd count it later.

Hastily she gathered her loot and plunged into her room. She had no traveling bags; no trunks! But then she realized she had no one to carry them anyway. In her largest reticule she could manage one change of clothes, the bottles, and a few toiletries, and that would be that. Fearfully she peered from the window, hoping not to see him, and then whirled into her work, stuffing into the reticule the bottles, a spare blue silk dress, petticoats, camisole, stockings, and the rest, not worrying about wrinkles. Then she pattered down the stairs into the strangely white parlor, blinking against the

sunlight. Her reticule weighed heavily on her shoulder and
that surprised her. Had she lost so much strength?

She slid outside, terrified of running into him, and chose
a roundabout path along the Tongue River. Soon she was
walking toward the station well concealed by trees, shrubs,
and river-front foliage. She'd done it. A tremble rattled
through her. He might yet discover her in town. Then what
would he do? He'd drag her back and plunge her into pure
hell. She tried to remember when the eastbound came. They
ran daily from the railhead at Livingston. Around noon, she
thought. She still had time.

She struck Main Street near Borchart's Corner and peered
sharply to the east, her eyes protesting against the white glare.
Two blocks away, near The Buffalo Hump Celebrity Hall, she
saw a small figure walking. Jubal. She ducked into the shadow
of a doorway and watched. She saw him cut north and disappear. Going home to the brick pile. He'd discover what she'd
done in a few minutes. He'd come looking. He'd get that little
secretary and comptroller of the company, Amos Howitzer,
and come looking. They'd find her. They'd try the train station
first. And the stagecoach offices second. And the hotels third.
Or maybe the livery, and question old Blue. It didn't matter.
They'd scour Miles City until they rooted her out.

If she went to the station one of the telegraphers, Neven
or Clewes, would gossip. Telegraphers were famous gossips.
The stationmaster, too. Or the ticket-seller. Suddenly she
hated what she'd done. She could just as well have stayed
quietly at the brick pile, bending to his cruelty and getting
her bottles somehow, one after another. How had she gotten
into this? It was that fraud of a funeral and then that pious
doctor. Or was he a sheriff? Toole confused her. But a thought
smoldered somewhere within her, waiting to ignite, and when
finally it did flare she knew she might find a haven, the one
spot Jubal Peach and Amos Howitzer would never look. A
place where she could wait until moments before the train
arrived, the wail of its whistle alerting her. She'd buy a ticket
on board and skip the station and the ticket window altogether.

The jail. She composed herself and stepped calmly out upon Main Street, the wide, muddy, rutted central thoroughfare of Miles City, lined now by boardwalks along the mercantiles and shops. She crossed the street, lifting her long skirt from the mud with her free hand, and paced quietly toward the tan stone building. She entered timidly—she'd never been in such a place—and found Toole's office empty and dark, and redolent with the smell of tobacco, gun oil, and the ash from the dead wood stove. Sunlight checkered the barren room, divided by barred windows. No one.

She sat in a wooden chair, peering fearfully out upon the bright street, afraid she'd be discovered after all. Toole would be at his practice now, mid-morning. She eyed the heavy, green-painted metal door at the rear, with its small barred window, the door into the cell room. Timidly she tried it and found it unlocked, which meant no one was incarcerated within. She pulled it, and the rank smell of urine and unnameable odors smacked her. She peered into the close, dark, cold air, seeing no one in any of the six cells. A terrible place, she thought. God help her if she ever had to spend time in such a place. She eyed the tin pails glinting dimly in each cell, and gagged. Nonetheless, all this was safety.

She entered, closing the heavy, squeaking door carefully behind her, and tiptoed to the darkest rear cell, wanting only silence and shadow. She found a hard bench in it and settled down, pained by the unyielding cold of the wood. No comfort. Even so she felt safe there, safe from Jubal's brutal clutch. She found a fresh bottle of Williams' in her reticule, uncorked it, and sucked desperately.

Jubal thought she was airing the house until he got to his bedroom and discovered the looted armoire. At that point he knew two things: She had all the juice, and he was going to run out shortly. He pushed back a panic that began to crawl through him, fed by the knowledge of what his body would do to him if it were deprived of its daily doses. He pulled his remaining bottle from his breast pocket and found it half-full. Enough for the moment. Relief flooded through him. He permitted himself a nip, so he could think straight.

Light blistered his dilated eyes. Not even his green celluloid spectacles abated the blinding roar of it, the chalky light that battered his room—all the rooms—and turned his own home into an alien cavern. He whipped the heavy drapes closed and fussed with them until the last bright ray vanished. Then he tackled her bedroom, finding it in disarray: chiffonier drawers gaping open, bedclothes tumbled. He pulled the heavy brocade drapes shut there, too, and raced downstairs. In a minute he had shut the intruding sun out of the rest of his house. It had pierced through windows as an alien force, evil and bright.

As soon as he'd restored the sepia darkness, he felt better. He could think. He settled into his horsehair parlor chair, pulled off his spectacles, studied on the matter. She'd fled somewhere, but not far. She wouldn't have the nerve to go far. Or would she? He raced upstairs and found the money gone, too. He'd been so intent on the missing bottles he'd forgotten. Maybe she meant to travel, after all. With his bottles. But he could catch her. She'd be cowering at the NP station, or some stagecoach office or freight depot. There weren't a lot of places she could hide in Miles City.

He felt better. He'd have those bottles back within an hour. As for her . . . he didn't know. Get her back here and then decide what to do. She'd become a useless thing, sulking around here, doing almost nothing. Maybe he'd put her on a train after all—without the juice. But he'd have to teach her manners, first. Southern ladies had manners. This woman needed instructing.

He'd have to deal with daylight again, so he donned his green spectacles and plunged into the bright morning, oblivious of the warm sun, fresh breeze, and dry air of late summer. He kept a sharp eye out for her as he hiked toward the Buffalo Hump, knowing he'd not see her. Main Street looked alive with morning commerce, but he knew he'd not find her in the mercantiles. He headed down Park, toward Professor Bach's Restaurant, where Amos Howitzer—as nocturnal as himself—would be having an eleven o'clock breakfast comprised of six ranch eggs, boiled potatoes, and a dill pickle.

Amos lounged in his usual corner, reading Frank Leslie's *Lady's Journal*, the fountain of most of his wisdom, and sipping coffee.

"Howitzer. We got a little business. Anna's fled the coop with my bottles."

Howitzer smiled gently. "You want the bottles."

"I want both."

"Alive or dead?"

"The bottles alive."

"When did this happen?"

"Sometime this morning. She's fixing to take the train. Or maybe a stage. Or if she had the brains she lacks, she'd latch onto a freight outfit. Anaway, you get the boys. I'm going to the station."

"To look for Anna?"

"That and wire Hartford. It'll take eight, ten days for more syrup to get here, Railway Express."

Howitzer grinned. "We'll have her in an hour."

"See to it."

Peach left the details to Howitzer, knowing the man would launch an intensive manhunt. Peach had half a dozen hardcases he could call on, each living in a small apartment at the rear of his several clubs. Like Howitzer these gents lived nocturnal lives, but he'd rouse them out and start them scouring Miles. One in particular, Clem Walden, would track her with the ruthlessness of a manhunter—which he'd once been until he accepted Peach's coin.

Peach hurried to the railroad station, the most likely place. He had business there in any case. Hour and a half before the eastbound arrived, so he had time. The oblong frame building lay on the south edge of town, on a loop off Pacific Avenue, just below the parlor houses of Sixth Street. He hurried past MacQueen House, the fancy hotel still under construction down there, the place where dudes fresh off the coaches headed and high-class types waited for the trains.

On a hunch he detoured into the lobby, studied everyone, and left. No Anna.

He plunged into the NP waiting room, assaulted by its odor of stale tobacco and varnish. No one. But of course Anna wouldn't loiter in plain sight. He trotted out to the platform and peered into the baggage room and the station-master's office. No Anna. He cut back to the telegraph office and found both Herold Neven and Fortney Clewes in residence.

"You seen my woman around?" he asked Clewes.

"No, Mr. Peach. Blonde, isn't she?"

"Take a wire. To Williams and Carleton, Hartford, Connecticut. Send four cases New England Cough Remedy via Railroad Express COD. And sign me. Got that, Clewes?"

The man in the green eyeshade scribbled it on a yellow pad, and accepted Jubal's double-eagle.

"Keep the change, Clewes."

The man nodded.

"Send that right away, and then tell me what else you got."

Clewes settled himself at the brass instrument and waited for it to stop chattering. Then, with a deft blur of fingers, he tapped out his message faster than Jubal's eyes could follow.

That was the main thing. Get more syrup. Maybe ten days. The possibility that they wouldn't find Anna alarmed him. He'd supposed it would be easy, but what if she had more brains than he'd thought? If she skipped, where would he get the juice he'd need to hold on? A ten-day wait would kill him.

Clewes approached the iron-barred window. "That's does it, Mr. Peach."

"Clewes. That woman's stolen half my goods, and I think she's running off. You going to be here a while?"

The telegrapher nodded.

Peach slid a ten-dollar greenback across the counter. "Will you send someone—a baggage man, anyone—if you spot her around here?"

"Sure will, Mr. Peach."

"What else you got for me?"

Clewes glanced at Neven, out of earshot and transcribing an incoming wire.

"A little. Couple days ago Toole wired General Cooke, in Denver City—Rocky Mountain Detective Association— asking for stuff on your man Howitzer."

"Why didn't you tell me right off?"

Clewes shrugged. "It ain't come back yet. Just thought I'd let you know, though. Sheriff's poking around."

"I want a flimsy when it comes. You make me a duplicate and I'll make you happy, Clewes."

The telegrapher smiled.

Peach stepped into the blazing sun again, hating it. Eleven-thirty. Howitzer would have all the boys out now, and they'd find her or not find her in minutes. All his clubs clustered in a small area. The Cottage Saloon, Brown's, The Keg, The Cosmopolitan Theatre and Saloon, all on a block or two of Main. Ward's Vaudeville and Chinnick's nearby. He walked north on Sixth Street, past the silent parlor houses that looked dead, or at least exhausted, in sunlight. Like the Buffalo Hump, he thought. They humped to life at night.

He passed The Stockman and smirked. It had stayed dark last night. He paused, peered into its gloomy interior, and saw chairs up on tables and gleaming floors. That Kate kept her joint polished up. Might be something to it, he thought. Anyway, he'd have the joint soon. Or at least keep it shut down. He reminded himself to stop at The Stockmen's and Drovers' Bank and do a little business. He knew the president. The president knew him. They always did business.

The thought of her upstairs, doing her books, coming up short, wondering how to pay Jubal the remaining hundred and seven, tickled him. He'd press her again, fast as he got Anna took care of. Maybe tonight.

The thought of Anna turned him uneasy again. He hastened to the Buffalo Hump, walked around to the rear door, and let himself in with his key. They'd report to him soon enough. In the blue dark he pulled his green spectacles off and tried to relax. He had a bunk there, but he settled into his quilted-leather swivel chair and stared into the gloom. He needed a dose, and pulled out his bottle. So little left. The thought appalled him, and he limited himself to a tiny sip of the sweet fluid. King of Miles City and a slave, he thought irritably. Anna's little escapade reminded him of it.

One by one over the next hour his men slipped in to report. Clem Walden had ransacked the stage stations, freight outfits, and the hotels for good measure. No Anna. Howitzer had studied every café in town and wandered through the mercantiles for good measure. No Anna. The rest of his saloon men had scoured the park, peered into Toole's cottage, the Bonus Dental Parlors, checked out the two livery barns, peered into empty freight cars on a siding—upsetting an NP rail dick—and had even checked the necessary rooms behind the lilac and chokecherry hedge at the rear of Peach's brick pile. No Anna.

"Keep looking," Peach commanded. "I want a watch on the depot, the stage offices, the freight outfits, and the livery barns."

"Someone's hiding her," Howitzer said.

"I'll rattle parlor house doors," Walden volunteered. "That's the only joints left."

"Anaway, there's a hunnert dollars for the one that gets her."

His men filed out. They'd get her. He had informants all over Miles, and they'd come to him. Meanwhile, though, he might run out of juice. It terrified him. No juice. His body tormented, like Anna's was all the time. But still, there were ways. Toole, for instance. Laudanum. Morphia. Paregoric. Anyway, enough to tide him over. He reached for his black bowler and pulled out his green spectacles.

Chapter 7

By noon Dr. Toole had ushered the last of his patients, old Folger Bass, out the door. Bass's consumption was staying quiescent, which pleased Santiago. He enjoyed the old mountain man.

Mimi summoned him to cabbage and corned beef. What wonders the railroad brought nowadays, he thought, digging in.

"She is a slave," Mimi said.

"Who?"

"Anna—the Peach woman yesterday morning."

"To opium, yes. Peach is, too."

"Not just that," Mimi said. "She's a slave to him. He stole her will from her."

"She might recover it, Mimi. She thought she saw her husband—her consort—being buried the other day. It tore her all to pieces."

Mimi gazed at him thoughtfully, her lustrous brown eyes absorbing it. "She can't escape. It's too late. She's dead but doesn't know it."

"I fear you're right."

"Poor thing," she whispered. "You'll help her if you can, Santo."

That was her way of requesting something. He smiled and polished off a delicious mound of corned beef.

His morning rounds had been cursory owing to the day's pressures, so he walked through a crisp, glowing, cool af-

ternoon toward his jail office. He'd pick up a nightstick there
and patrol the West End in the fine, sage-scented air.

That's where Jubal Peach found him.

It astonished Santiago. That night owl, Peach, had wandered into the sheriff's office in the middle of the day, looking
reasonably chipper in spite of the odd hours he kept. Opiates
could do that, he thought. Only Jubal Peach didn't look opiated; indeed, he seemed nervous and taut as piano wire.

"Peach! I take it you broke Miss Dubois's bank."

"Oh, yeah. Anaway, Toole, have you seen the woman?"

"Miss Kate?"

"No, the little woman."

Sudden caution swept through Santiago. Indeed, he had
seen her yesterday, and she'd seemed desperate. "Why do
you ask, Peach?"

Something hooded slipped over the gambler's face. "Oh,
just looking. She's around somewheres. I thought to have her
fix me a plate."

"She's not home, I take it."

"I got Howitzer looking. Strange, is all."

He hung there, nervously, not leaving. From west of town
the wail of the arriving eastbound NP passenger train echoed
through the office, and presently its chuffing thunder.

"Say, while I'm here," said Peach. "I'm feeling a lot of
aches and rheumatiz and the ague off and on—southerners
don't take to this climate well. And I was thinking . . . I
could use some anodynes. For two weeks, anaway."

Toole stared sharply at Peach. The man who was awash
in opiates wanted an anodyne. "Well," he began cautiously,
"I'm not sure you need any. Bed rest does wonders."

"Toole, don't. I want an anodyne."

"All right. I'll give the alcoholic extract of henbane, *hy-
osycamus niger*, quite powerful, good for allaying pain,
calming the mind. It doesn't constipate, either, the way opiates do. Two grains would do you."

"Not that, Toole. I want the other. Laudanum, Paregoric,
Dover's Powder." Something strident rang in Peach's voice.

That was it, then, Santiago thought. Peach had run out of

his narcotic cough syrup. Run out—or had it stolen from him. The thought suddenly intrigued him: Anna.

"I don't have all day, Toole."

Santiago thought swiftly. Men as addicted as Peach would kill or rob for the narcotic they needed. No sense letting that happen.

"Have you ever thought of cutting back, Peach? A little less each day?"

"I don't want lectures, Toole."

Santiago sighed and dug into his Gladstone, finding a half-filled blue bottle there. "Here's some laudanum. It should last you."

Peach grabbed it, his hand trembling. "This isn't two weeks, Toole."

"What's left is for medical emergencies, people in pain."

"How fast can you get more—by wire?"

"From the Twin Cities, three days by train."

"Get some. I'll pay well."

"You've lost your supply."

"Something like that."

"Mind telling me what happened? If it was stolen, that's a crime and I'm here to look into it."

"No, nothing. Just misplaced—an order didn't come in."

"I'll look into it," Santiago said.

"No you won't."

Santiago sighed. He had a fair idea what had happened. "That'll be two for the consultation, six for the laudanum, Peach."

The gambler dug into his frock coat and peeled a ten from a roll of greenbacks.

"I'll get the change to you," Santiago said.

Peach whirled out, paused on the jail portico, and lifted the blue bottle to his lips. Two blocks away the NP eastbound chuffed and screeched and rolled slowly out of Miles, its single green-and-gilt coach sooty in the melancholy sun.

Santiago stood at his barred window, peering out upon the man who wished to be King of Miles City but was a slave to opium. A man looking for his woman, as he called her. Anna

Waldevsky, who no doubt had every drop of the Williams' New England Cough Remedy that Peach had stashed away somewhere.

It intrigued him. What was she doing? Had there been a crime? Was she still in Miles, and in danger? Left on that train he could still hear rattling eastward? He feared for her, suddenly. That could be a killing matter, making off with an addict's opium supply. Peach had been evasive about it. But plainly desperate. There he was, running her to ground when he should have been in bed. And Howitzer, too. Running down Anna—to do what?

Santiago sighed, thinking he'd better slip his black belt with its heavy holstered burden around his waist and see what he could see—and prevent, if it came to that.

That's when he heard the cell room door creak open. He whirled, black Remington in hand, and saw her there, behind the swinging door. He sighed, felt a huge pulse throb through him and convulse his limbs and fingers.

"That explains it."

She looked guilty and frightened.

"I was going to catch the train. But I couldn't."

She slid fearfully into the front office, peering sharply out the barred window, light and shadow crisscrossing her jaundiced, yellow-gray flesh.

Santiago eased himself slowly into his hard wooden chair, uncomfortable.

"I took your advice. I want to escape."

"With his bottles."

She nodded unhappily. "Enough for two months, maybe. I could get a job, earn enough to buy them. Back home."

"Where's that, Miss Waldevsky?"

"Kansas City. I think they'd let me come home."

"You haven't really escaped, you know."

She looked alarmed. "He'll find me. He'll drag me out of here."

"Not that, Anna. You haven't escaped the bottles."

"I don't want to."

It always came to that, he thought. Slavery. "You're welcome to stay back there if you want. It's a full day until the next eastbound, though. Westbound leaves tonight, a quarter to ten.''

She peered at him fearfully. ''Will I be safe?''

''No. Howitzer or Peach—I take it they're hunting for you—will check here. I could lock the cell room door, lock you in. But you wouldn't like that. And they still might spot you if they peer in.''

''I can't bear to be locked up.''

''I can do this, Anna: Lock the front door of my office when I leave. You won't be locked in. Just turn the bolt when you want to get out. But they can't get into this office or peer back into the cell room.''

''Oh, I'd like that.''

''You'll need food.''

She shook her head. ''I'm not hungry.''

He sighed. Addicts usually weren't. ''They'll be watching the station when the westbound comes in. Also the eastbound tomorrow. And the coaches. Have you any plan?''

She shook her head. ''I just did it. I didn't think.''

''I have an idea,'' he said. ''A place where you'd be safe for a few days, until they quit looking for you.'' He peered at her sternly. ''You're not married?''

''No.''

''If you are, I'd be duty-bound to return you to your husband. One more thing: Did you damage anything?''

She nodded. ''His armoire. I broke the door with a crowbar.''

He wondered about it. A common-law wife taking things from a common-law husband; breaking furniture, too. ''You go back there, then. I want to talk with someone, if I can.''

She slipped timidly into the cell room while he pulled on his black hat and started for Miss Kate's, hoping she was awake.

Kate Dubois slept through the afternoon and the night and awoke the next morning. She felt better. Her first act was to reach for the ivory-handled looking glass on her bedside table so that she might examine herself.

She'd never been quite satisfied with her face, but generally conceded it wasn't all that bad. She could never find the faintest sign of crow's feet or other aging in her twenty-six-year-old features. She didn't particularly like her jawline, thought it a bit sharp, and her eyebrows seemed a tiny bit too low, her neck a shade long. But she knew how to deal with those things, so that she always seemed a willowy beauty in the eyes of admiring men. For another ten years or so her beauty would be better than possessing diamonds or sapphires. After that she'd prefer the gemstones. But for the time being her beauty would be her salvation.

Now she gazed into the looking glass, and it revealed dark hollows under her eyes and an unhealthy gray in her flesh. She wondered if she remained ill, felt her forehead, and knew herself to be cured of whatever small fever had beset her. Dr. Toole's Dover's Powder had slid her into a long and therapeutic sleep. Tonight she would reopen the saloon. Perhaps she would even operate her games, with strict maximum limits. She'd know better when she got through the afternoon. She felt confident that she could borrow five hundred dollars from various merchants—enough for a small bank, if she kept her wagering limits low.

They'd lend it to her, a hundred here, two hundred there, and their wives would scold. She smiled softly. In the beau monde she'd fled, wives and mistresses didn't scold. If anything, they were all more beautiful than Kate, selected and possessed for their clean-limbed grace and patrician confidence. But it wasn't really *her* beau monde. Her mother was a live-in maid. Kate had grown up among the very rich, but not as one of them. She'd never known her father and her mother had never mentioned him, so Kate thought she probably was a bastard. She'd grown up penniless in a great Newport, Rhode Island, mansion, absorbing everything, resenting everything—and growing nubile in her own right.

In the world she had hovered around, women knew how to paint themselves gorgeous, how to deal with small flaws of face and form, how to wear their hair and make their eyes large. They knew how to walk and stand, and speak with dulcet voices. How to flirt and meet a gaze boldly. How to say yes while saying no. They knew just what to say to wreathe a man's face in smiles, when to be the coquette and when the serene matron. They were superior to fashion and wore what suited them rather than what was the rage of Paris. She herself had learned all the things that the rich learned: to sail, play whist and croquet, and ride hot-blooded horses astride. Young bluebloods noticed her, tried to seduce her, and when that failed tried to make her their mistress. But they never proposed. Not to a maid's daughter. She had only to surrender to live out the rest of her days in luxury, and even acquire wealth of her own. But she had refused.

She could have become a rich man's possession. Bought and paid for to show off. Beautiful women were the mark of a man's success. Let him accumulate a modest pile and he could have an empty beauty. Let him accumulate millions and he could buy a delicious, daring vamp who could make men faint of heart and kindle hunger in their eyes. Kate's memories stopped there, reviewing that part of it, the part that had stirred dark rebellion while she was still a budding girl; the part that had, in the end, catapulted her out into the wide world under an assumed name. Those who wished to possess her never found her and never would. The very thought of one young blueblood in particular raised her hackles even now, years later.

Lulu brought her tea in pink Wedgwood bone china, the pot steaming and the cup brimming with liquid the color of alfalfa honey.

"You are better, Miss Kate."

"I'll be up directly. The lemon silk today, Lulu."

The graying woman nodded.

"And a bath."

"We've started the water heating, Miss Kate."

Twenty minutes later Kate Dubois was easing her slim white form into a claw-legged iron tub, enameled white, with a dark-stained oaken rim around the top. Lulu sudsed her hair with lilac-scented Castile, rinsed it carefully with fresh warm water, and left her to her own devices. Kate loved to bathe. And she loved to think while she bathed. The warmth stimulated her mind.

She wiggled her toes. She had perfect feet and calves, a fact known only to herself. She might take the war to Jubal and do unto him what he had just done unto her. It wouldn't be easy with a small bank, and borrowed at that. Not that the merchants would want repayment. That was the thing about beauty. Men rushed to do things for her.

Jubal would be at his faro layout as usual and sucking up his opium, as usual. She could not break his bank but she could renew her own, perhaps. She could try faro, or propose poker. But no, that was a bad idea. In addition to going against his house odds she'd be going against the crookedest mountebank west of the Mississippi. Some thought faro was foolproof and square, but she knew better. Nothing compelled a dealer to pull the top two cards off the deck when he reached into the slot in the case box. Poker would be as bad. Peach wore a mirror ring, and the headlight diamond in his cravat had a large flat facet, just right for reading the cards he dealt. And the deck itself would be braced.

No. She wouldn't enter his lair.

Still, she had to do something. If she didn't take the fight to him, she'd be done for. He'd find some way to finish what he'd started. She'd been broke before but not like this, not with debt hovering over her, and responsibilities. Poverty lurked dangerously, like a slinking tiger. It occurred to her she might go hungry, fail to pay on her mortgage, fail to pay her help what she owed, be evicted, put out on the streets. It vaguely excited her, this lurking tiger. She'd fled west to live life to the hilt, unfettered by men, and now she'd either succeed or lose the dream.

Her water had grown cold. She stood, feeling it trickle coolly from her, and then toweled herself. She slipped into her canary cotton wrapper and settled in the rosewood settee next to her south window, where the brilliant high-plains sun would dry her shoulder-long hair swiftly. In an hour she could pile it into a bun and venture out.

While she waited she manicured her nails and pondered. There wasn't a lot she could do about Jubal Peach except shoot him. She could keep him out of her club; Peach and all his men. But only if Sheriff Toole helped her. Once, Peach had planted a mob of toughs and bullyboys on the boardwalk just in front of her place. They forced her patrons to run a gauntlet of clenched fists and insults until Toole arrived. He had surveyed the hooligans quietly and didn't even try to disperse them while they jeered at him. Instead, he'd trotted over to the Buffalo Hump and arrested Peach and shut The Buffalo Hump Celebrity Palace down. He had kept Peach in the jail for several hours and let him out on the promise that he'd never harry Miss Kate's customers again. Peach had left in a rage but he'd called his dogs off. It could happen again, she thought.

She folded her hair into a bun while it was still a bit damp and slid the black velvet choker with the pineapple cameo around her throat. Smashing, she thought. Glimmering ash-blond hair, yellow ribbon, bold gray eyes, high-necked canary-colored summer dress of Irish linen.

She found Sylvane Tobias, in a blue bib apron, building a casket of oak plank. He peered up from his planing, his bulky, varicosed face surveying her uneasily, and set down his plane.

"Sylvane," she said, "Jubal broke the bank."

"So I've heard.'

"Who's that for?" she asked, pointing at the lidless box.

"Maybe you," he said dourly.

"Sylvane!"

"From what I hear you'd be smart to sell for whatever you can and pull out."

"I'm not going anywhere. That's what I came to see you about . . ."

"Howitzer and two others came by. Day after the funeral. Told me Jubal wasn't a bit pleased. Said if I ever crossed

Jubal again, I'd be fish food. I reckon your being pretty doesn't slow Jubal down a bit. You'd just be pretty fish food.''

Tobias pulled curls of blond wood from his plane and began working the edge of the plank again.

''Sylvane, I'd like to borrow money. Two hundred if possible. For a new bank.''

''No.''

''I'm good for it, Sylvane. The club earns steadily and I have loyal patrons—because I'm square.''

''Because you're a looker,'' he grunted. ''No. You ain't reckoning on Jubal Peach. You think that funeral we did was just a joke, like thumbing your nose. To him, it meant more. He took it bad enough to send Howitzer after me. No. I lend you money for a bank and I'd fill that box there.''

''He'd never know.''

Tobias glared. ''There's a mighty short list of people in Miles who'd lend you a bank. Me and Gatz, Huffman, Blue at the livery barn, maybe one or two more.''

She smiled. ''I'll find it somewhere. I was going to offer you more than interest. Interest and a cut of the profits for a while, until it's paid.''

''No,'' he said. ''You'd best forget it. Hate to drive a lady like you up the hill.''

''Thanks anyway, Sylvane.''

He returned to his planing and she left, feeling his eyes on her back. It had been a novelty for her, being turned down.

Chapter 8

No bank. Kate had prayed to the merchants and none of them would lend her anything. Mrs. Gatz had been feather-dusting a can of Dr. LeGear's Poultry Wormer Powder when Kate had waltzed into the store, and when she'd approached Horton he refused her curtly, his gaze sliding off to his hood-eyed, thin-lipped wife. The others had dealt with her much the same way.

She might be respectable in her own eyes, she thought, but to them she was one of the sporting people, one of the demimonde. And her dazzle hadn't helped her at all. She sensed it had defeated her. They didn't trust her; didn't believe they'd ever fish their principal back, much less turn a profit on it. And she tapped yet another undercurrent: they feared Jubal Peach. Or at least they feared the forces Peach could unloose upon Miles, the things that a man such as Amos Howitzer could do.

She turned wearily back toward The Stockman, aware of the people on the street who studied her curiously, admired her mysterious aura, eyed an unraveling seam running from the armpit to the waist of her lemon-yellow suit that exposed Chantilly lace underneath, and gave her affectionate smiles on the gritty plank sidewalks. Let them see lace, she thought. She returned each smile, but her soul brimmed with memories of her childhood, a life lived among the cavalier. Sometimes a democratic impulse seized them and then she might enjoy their company—for a few hours. Other times, though, they had casually shut her out, as if she were an invisible waif, scarcely present at their teas and croquet and lemon-aded lawn parties, a sort of mosquito netting separating her from them. That feeling swept her now, the sense of being separated by some kind of gauze from the rest of the world. It had formed her. Made her keep her distance, even though she loved those around her and could never have enough of their company.

When she reached the Sporting District she didn't want to go on. She stopped, watching a tumbleweed somersault across the wide, rutted road. A great sense of emptiness hollowed her chest. What was she doing here? It had seemed a good business proposition: cowboys, soldiers, brakemen, all footloose, unattached, and ready to blow their pay. She stared hard, seeing a squalid, raw town she'd never seen before. The hills lay yellow and empty, shorn even of their dun grasses by overgrazing. Pewter sagebrush, the color of dry moss, choked the bottoms of distant coulees. The Sporting District she'd called home for two years slouched in chalky sun, looking grimy and exhausted. And lonely. Men came for sport, for gambling and drink, and left penniless and alone, sucked dry by people like herself who offered counterfeit joy. But was it counterfeit? Had she offered only that?

Something sagged in her. Maybe she should go. Escape this desolate outpost. Turn it over to Jubal Peach and his kind. Everything here was barbarous. She'd brought a touch of gentility to the West End. She'd made The Stockman solid and discreet, and then added a bit of grandeur for fun. Like Itzak Ugurplu's black livery. The thought of him filled her with melancholy. She loved them all dearly. Boris, Lulu, Eddie Duquesne, two bartenders, three other table men, a swamper—she couldn't pay. She knew they'd sacrifice for her; work for nothing but the hustle if she let them. But with no bank in sight her prospects had collapsed. She'd bucked her own tiger.

She paused at the boot-battered doors of her establishment, not wanting to go in, her soul yearning for the sweets that could not be. Just then she gladly would have traded it, given up the sporting life, for the embrace of a strong, gentle, good man. Like Dr. Toole. Not that he was such a catch. She didn't think much of the Irish. Too sentimental. And even less of aristocrats and exiles and Catholics. She put him out of mind. Between herself and Dr. Toole there hung not one but a dozen veils of mosquito netting, his layers, his protection against her. She'd seen it in his eyes when he'd examined her, seen the spastic movement of his hands and body, seen his eyes focus on the ivory- and rose-flowered wallpaper. That's how it always was with respectable men, and she wouldn't even consider the other kind. She smelled alkali dust in the breeze, hated it suddenly, and fled inside into the only world she had, feeling lonely.

She opened The Stockman that evening, but only the saloon. She draped muslin sheets over the games in the club room but left the door open and the back room lantern-lit—just in case Sheriff Toole got fussy about enforcing the town ordinances. The round, green-baize poker tables she left uncovered. She couldn't play but others could, and they'd order drinks while playing. She barely had ten dollars for bar change and still owed Peach a hundred and seven. And she'd need to replenish her Kentucky soon to keep on going.

Not many sports showed up at first. They eyed the sheet-shrouded gaming tables mournfully, as if studying the deceased, and then bought a two-bit whiskey or a mug of Bullard's. But she knew her trade would increase soon, when word got around that Miss Kate's double doors had opened again. Old Boris perched on a stool at the rear, his bent frame encased in boiled shirt and black frock coat. He'd hung his Czarina Catherina silver medallion from his creased neck, suspended this evening upon a water-shot purple ribbon so that he looked like a wine steward. In his ancient hands it made a fine knout, and Catherine's profile had indented many a skull, as had the peace dove on the obverse side. Eddie Duquesne and Itzak Ugurplu had come too, even though she'd tried to shoo them away and had told them she couldn't pay them a dime.

She wore her most daring dress, black velveteen with a bodice that drew stares. If she couldn't offer faro she could offer dreams, she'd thought. But it had been a mistake, she now realized. They'd come to sympathize, these few patrons, and her white décolleté drew dour glances. This woman wasn't the Miss Kate they'd known. At last, embarrassed, she retreated to her rooms and changed into her usual demure, high-necked, puff-sleeved blouse, stiff dark skirt, and her hallmarked black velvet choker, this time suspending a jade-and-ivory cameo with a scrimshawed cat on it. When she returned she sensed pleasure in their glances. She felt pleased and chastened.

But no one talked. A stupefying quiet gripped The Stockman, like people waiting for a Requiem Mass to begin. Her place remained mute and dumb until around ten, when Amos Howitzer wandered in, peered steadily at the patrons, and headed for the bar, his dented derby bobbing on his square head.

She intercepted him. "I'm sorry, Mr. Howitzer. Not here."

He ignored her and pressed into the rosewood bar.

"Beer," he said.

She shook her head. "The Stockman is not open to Mr. Peach and his people."

He looked at her, amused, his eyes roving down her figure.

"Beer," he said. The barman, Portneuf, blinked.

Old Boris had unfolded from his stool and creaked toward them. Howitzer's gaze, inscrutable in the lantern light, followed him.

"Mr. Howitzer, the lady has spoken."

Amos Howitzer stood frozen, measuring the odds, and then sagged slightly. "I've come for the hunnert and seven. You promised it."

"Mr. Peach will get it. But not tonight."

"Now."

"In a week."

"The boss will take measures."

"You may not get it at all."

"I'll have a beer."

"You heard Miss Dubois," said Boris.

"I see her violatin' the ordinance."

Scarcely had he said this than Sheriff Toole pushed through the heavy doors and stood there, absorbing the scene.

Howitzer smirked. For a moment Kate thought the pair of them had conspired. She straightened herself and stood unmoving, awaiting whatever would come.

As he approached the bar Toole eyed her, studied Howitzer, noted old Boris glowering beside them.

"You've opened," he said. "Without the games."

"Go ahead," she snapped. "I'll get a lawyer. I'm going to tell Pericles Shaw the owner of a business has a right to . . . to manage it."

Santiago grinned. "Whoa up. What're you jabbering about, Miss Dubois?"

"She ain't sposed to be in here," Howitzer said.

"I gather you're not either, Howitzer."

"She's asked him to leave—twice," growled Boris.

"Then you'd better leave. Her place, isn't it, Howitzer?"

"Make me, Sheriff."

Toole's hickory nightstick cracked Howitzer across the side of his right knee. And again.

"Aoww!" Howitzer screamed, and fainted. Kate watched the burly man sag to the floor and land in a heap.

Boris smiled softly, respect in his rheumy eyes.

"But . . . how?" asked Kate.

"Most painful blow known to man," Santiago said. "Want to feel it?"

On the jack pine sawdust Howitzer rolled and groaned. Santiago stooped, patted the man, slid from various twill recesses a Beals revolver, a woven leather blackjack, and a folding knife, and handed them to Boris.

"Business is slow this evening, Miss Kate?"

"I'm open. Maybe word will get around. Are you arresting me?"

"What for?"

From the floor Howitzer said, "For being in here."

"I think that ordinance doesn't apply to owners."

"Who says?"

Toole smiled down at him. Slowly Howitzer sat up, rubbing his aching knee, sawdust and dirt flaking off of his gray gabardine.

"I didn't know about that one," he muttered. He retrieved his sawdust-caked derby and stood shakily. "That's the worst I've ever known. I'm going to try that."

"Miss Kate asked you to leave," Santiago said. "And don't come back. Your instruments of death will be sent over to the Buffalo Hump in the morning."

They watched Howitzer limp out.

"Let's have a talk, lass," he said, motioning her back toward the empty club room. She followed him doubtfully, wondering when he'd haul her off to the jail. She'd never been arrested. She was becoming less and less sure about living on the edge.

"I need your help," he said softly. "I need to hide someone for a few days."

She stared.

"I mean a woman," he muttered. "Peach's woman."

Five minutes later, she agreed. "I could have Lulu put a tick upstairs for Anna Waldevsky, until the woman could safely catch a train out.

"If I'm still open," she added. "With this light saloon trade I can't last even a few days, Sheriff."

"I'll look for a bank," he replied.

"You'll look for a bank?"

"You're as good as Drexel, Morgan and Company."

She found his eyes on her but couldn't look up at him, and when she forced herself to it was through a blur.

He rotated the wick upward, scratched a match and lit it, and lowered it again. Then he dropped the glass chimney in place and walked through the cell room to the iron cubicle at the rear. The bars made bobbing tiger stripes on the lamplit walls. He found her huddled on the hard bench, her skirts tucked tight against the cold, her bony fingers clutching a brown rectangular bottle.

"I have a safe place," he said.

Anna peered up at him dully from dilated eyes. With all those bottles at hand she'd gone on a spree, he realized.

She nodded and sat.

"Come along."

She didn't do anything at all.

He lifted her by the arm and she followed passively, her heavy bag burdening her. He closed the cell room door behind them and extinguished his lamp. His office blued into blackness, and he smelled the char of the dying wick. He peered out upon Main Street, seeing no one. But the evening was young and he had to be careful. Her dull blond hair would give her away.

He hurried her across Main and then south, into an alley. He intended to approach The Stockman from the rear. She followed passively. He eyed her unhappily, wondering just what he was inflicting on Kate Dubois. He threaded back alleys through a carbonous night, scaring up cats and skunks. At last he cut to the right and halted at the looming rear wall of The Stockman, charred where Peach's arsonist had started a coal-oil blaze. He knocked. Lulu opened and nodded in the amber glow.

"This is Anna Waldevsky. She's, ah, indisposed," he said.

The ample old woman eyed Peach's blonde shrewdly and took her in hand, about the way one would touch a leper.

"Thank you. And thank Miss Dubois."

Lulu glared at him and shut the door with a thud. He stood quietly, alert for spectators, but sensed none. Howitzer would be over at the Buffalo Hump, nursing his knee.

A bank for Kate. He had a notion, but didn't quite know the angle of attack. He slipped out upon Main, listened to a tinny piano, watched a few noncoms pause, undecided, arguing about where to lose their coin. He turned toward the center of town, checking the scabrous doors of the merchant establishments as he walked. At the log courthouse he cut straight across yards and emerged a block north on Seventh, at a squat wood rectangle of a bungalow with a pyramidal sheet-metal roof. Lamplight pewtered a wavery glass pane full of minute bubbles.

He knocked. Pericles T. Shaw opened. The justice of the peace wore a buffalo coat, its brown curly hair turning him bearish. Beneath, bare calves and hammertoed feet projected downward like varicosed celery stalks.

"Contempt of court," he said. "What do you want?"

"Investments, Pericles."

"I'm reading Gibbon. *The Decline and Fall* has lessons, Toole. I'm at Justinian. A heretic. Codifier of the *corpus juris civilis*, Roman law. His wife Theodora was the daughter of a circus man and an actress and slut. What do you want, a warrant?"

"Money," said Toole.

"If you'd bring me more crooks, I'd have more fines. You're lax."

Santiago followed the justice into his parlor and lowered himself onto a settee while Shaw settled into his enormous brown horsehair chair. A taffy-colored hound licked Shaw's toes.

"Not public money. Your money."

"It's all one and the same, except what the commissioners gouge out of me."

"Miss Kate needs a bank."

Shaw peered up alertly, his bulldog jowls flapping. "So I've heard."

"It'd be good for the town. Keep Peach from gaining a monopoly on vice."

"That's the wrong tack."

"You could lend it at good rates."

"That's a better tack. Not sure I have anything to lend."

"You have thousands."

"Why would I supply Miss Kate with a bank?"

"It's an aesthetic proposition."

Pericles agreed, nodding slowly. "What would keep the sun shining upon Miles City?"

"Five hundred. Payable in six months at eight percent, or ten percent of the profits for a year, such as they may be."

"What is her surety?"

"Her face."

"Hmmm. If I tried to borrow on my face, you'd nip me for a thimblerigger."

"That's true, Pericles."

"I have a pixy and adventuresome character, Toole. It's a weakness."

"I'm exploiting it."

"And felonious impulses. It will cost her a stolen kiss."

"I doubt she'll yield, Pericles."

"Bring her around tomorrow, Toole. I'll be shooting flies after nine."

"I'll bring her." Toole rose.

"You can find your way to the door. I wish to see how Justinian reconciles the Monophysites before I surrender."

The hound followed him to the door and lifted a leg as he shut it. Toole struck for home, an evening's work behind him.

He found Mimi under the down quilt.

"You're early, Santo."

"I did a good evening's work. And it's quiet tonight."

He lit a bedside lamp and tugged at his black frock coat. She watched him.

"I found a place to hide poor Anna Waldevsky."

She waited, her brown eyes lustrous in the brassy light.

"At The Stockman. That's the one place Peach can't reach her. Kate will look after her until Peach's punks quit watching the stations."

"Now it's Kate," she said.

Oblivious, Santiago went on with his tale. "She's opened the saloon. Not much trade, though. Sheets over the tables, except poker. I told her I'd help her get a bank."

"You *what*, Santiago?" Mimi sat up in bed, glaring at him.

"I talked to Pericles about a bank. She couldn't get one from the storekeeps."

"They're smart," she snapped. "Also, they've got wives." She let that hang, but he ignored it and unlaced his hightop shoes.

"Hate to have her leave town."

"Hate to have her leave! Is that what you think? Is she prettier than I am?"

"She's beautiful, Mimi. Ethereal, in some strange way."

"What'd she offer you for a bank, Santiago Toole?"

He grinned. "Tears."

"I knew it was something. She weeps two tears and every man in town leaps. If I cried, would you find a bank for me?"

"You're even more beautiful, Mimi."

In fact, she was. She'd washed her hair, and it hung black and gilded in the amber light, sliding over her shoulders in thick dark waves. Her honey flesh glowed above the white ruffle of her thin nightgown, and the high Assiniboin bones under her eyes turned her oriental.

She watched him slit-eyed, like an angry cat.

"And I love you, lass."

"More than her?"

He laughed.

Mimi pulled the comforter aside and said scornfully, "Protestants don't know how to make love. Neither do white women. Except the French. She might be beautiful, but Venus is nothing but a marble statue, Santo."

Santiago didn't wait.

Chapter 9

Toole visited Kate early in the afternoon. She rarely awakened before noon, and her day had scarcely begun. She threaded her way down the dark stairs and into the gloomy saloon, empty and quiet and smelling of fresh pine sawdust on the plank floor. Boris had let him in.

He stood quietly, wearing his black vest with no frock coat. Hot out, she thought. His steel star glowed dully in the subdued light.

"Sheriff?" she said, extending a hand.

"How's Miss Waldevsky?"

"I scarcely know. I just got up. Lulu made a bed for her in the alcove. Sleeping, I suppose. If you'd call it that."

Toole nodded. "I have to take you before the justice of the peace."

Something cold lanced through her. "You're doing it, then? Because I was present in my own business?"

He nodded solemnly.

"But . . . you said . . ." A rage began building in her. "Have you arrested Peach—and his serving women?"

"No," Toole admitted.

"So this is Miles City justice."

Toole nodded again.

"How am I supposed to pay? I'm penniless! I suppose it'll be fun to lock me up!"

Toole smiled.

"Who'll run this place? How much is the fine? How long—"

"Pericles Shaw will decide all that."

She knew she shouldn't say it but it welled up in her and exploded over her tongue. "Peach owns you!"

He blinked. "I wouldn't say that," he muttered. "That's a serious accusation."

"I don't care! Fine me for that, too! The town's owned by a crook and his . . . lackeys."

"Pericles will find you in contempt, Miss Dubois."

"I don't care about that, either! All right, take me!"

He nodded. They slipped out to the bright street, into a furnace wall of heat. She retreated into herself as they walked east, disappointment lacing her. Toole either had been bought or he was an ass. In either case she would be finished here. The Stockman would collapse. She'd be lucky to scrape up a railroad ticket to somewhere else. Anywhere. She now hated this rough, ill-kempt, dreary prairie outpost anyway.

At least he hadn't manacled her or shamed her, she thought, seeing ranch women on the street. She fumed as they walked, hotter than the oppressive dry air around her, bitterness tightening her chest. She'd tongue-lash that squat, smelly JP, too, and the hell with the consequences.

"I just did you a favor, too," she muttered.

"Not me. Miss Waldevsky."

"Peach's woman. This whole thing smells. Next thing, Peach will bust into my place and take her and you'll have me on kidnapping charges, too."

"Could be."

The answer didn't comfort her. The awesome heat wilted her and moistened her armpits, but she wouldn't let him see it. Her blue gingham would be soaked soon. Maybe the jail would be cool. People said the cells were cold.

"How could you?"

"Oh, I could," he said. "I could. I do what's right for Miles City."

"Right for Miles City! Destroy the last independent club, the last place customers can come for an honest game and a good drink. Close it down so Peach has no real competition, so they can all play with his braced decks and swill down his red-eye. Now he'll be king. Opium is what'll be king! Everything he does is drugged by that stuff he drinks."

Toole nodded. He didn't even seem worried about it. He just walked along as if he deserved respect, as if he had a clean soul, as if he were a virtuous man instead of a corrupt lackey. A crook. A doctor who was a crook.

"You disappoint me."

"We do what we have to."

They turned into the flagstoned courthouse walk, which led to a rough log building with whitewash peeling from it like mange. From within the muffled boom of a shot pummeled her ears.

"Don't mind that," Toole said. "He likes to slaughter flies while he holds court."

She'd heard about it. The JP had an ancient revolver on his bench, which he used as a gavel. He loaded it with small charges of powder and a bit of sand wrapped in cigarette paper, turning it into a tiny shotgun.

Toole steered her into the stark room, which smelled of ancient spit and cigars and powder smoke. A deafening blast met them.

"Hold still," Pericles Shaw commanded.

"Pericles! Don't aim it—"

Another blast, and Kate felt sand smack her shoes.

"Contempt of court," Pericles Shaw said, in his gravelly voice. "What you got here, Sheriff? I haven't seen anything so pretty around here in months. You should pinch her more often."

"This is Kate Dubois, Mr. Justice."

He scrutinized her through tiny half glasses from his seat above. His gaze pierced so deeply she felt as if he'd plumbed her soul and read her mind.

"Hold on a moment," he muttered, and leveled the battered revolver at a monarch butterfly that had drifted through the open window, a radiant orange-and-black beauty. The blast rattled Kate's ears. The gossamer creature was blown into fragments and fluttered to the gritty planks below.

"Oh!" she cried. "You beast!"

"Contempt of court," he said, banging his revolver.

She loathed him, loathed the white jowls that flapped as he spoke, loathed his squat toad shape, his balding head, his small mean eyes behind those tiny spectacles.

"I know your kind!"

"Do you, now? Are you God?"

Shaw rattled her. She subsided into resentful quiet, afraid she'd get herself in worse trouble. She didn't even have a lawyer to help her, and no money to pay one, anyway.

"This is a lawful court, Miss Dubois," Toole said.

"I grew up among people with great power—and money. But I had none. I know what they do to others. They do it unthinkingly sometimes, but they do it," she said softly. "What is a single defenseless woman to do? You tear my life apart. I've lived honorably, but it doesn't matter. I believe in—I have ideals, but it doesn't matter. I'm a woman alone, a woman making her way without help from men, and doing it in a way that—" She sagged, the burden of all this suddenly more than she could bear. "I'm in your way," she muttered. "I'm in Peach's way. I'm the last obstacle to you all. Go ahead and do what you will."

She thought she caught an expression of misgiving in Shaw's eye. At least he had turned solemn. He read a lot, she knew. Maybe she had touched something in him.

"What's the charge, Toole?"

"Vagrancy. She's without visible means."

Kate couldn't believe her ears. "Vagrancy! Vagrancy! Why you low-down crooked—"

"That's worth five hundred. Eight percent interest per year," Shaw rasped. He gaveled the bench with the butt of the old revolver. It boomed, blowing a load of sand into his stained water-shot waistcoat. "It always does that," he muttered.

"Five hundred—for vagrancy?" She felt the last fragments of her will disintegrate. Miles City had claimed her. Old Boris could never get her out. Lawyers couldn't wrest her from this. She'd spend months in that awful jail. . . . She knew better than to argue. What was vagrancy worth? A two-dollar fine and an order to leave town? Five hundred! Proof. She stared first at Toole, feeling a sadness about him, about this amiable man turned crook, and then at the judge, gray and toadlike above.

"I can't pay it," she whispered.

"You're good for it. Your, ah, beauty will see you through. Would eight percent be acceptable?"

"Are you saying . . . ." Was that old goat suggesting . . . ?

"Yes, you're good for it," Shaw said, blinking down at her.

"But I don't have it."

"Of course not. But you'll get it, soon as you reopen the club room."

"I can't do that."

"With a bank you can. Not all the games, but your faro, and maybe another."

She sighed. Behind her she heard a door closing and then she saw Boris enter. The old man looked stern. At least she wasn't alone and this travesty would be witnessed, she thought.

"Boris! They've got me on vagrancy! And it's five hundred dollars."

Voroshlikov looked shocked.

Shaw drummed his revolver on the bench. It echoed in the bare courtroom. "Order in the court! Defendant will not talk to spectators."

She bit back a whole lava flow of invective. Never had she been so much at the mercy of the powerful.

The JP set his revolver down, bore aimed out at old Boris, licked a finger, and began counting money. She watched, puzzled, as his rubbery white fingers tugged at greenbacks.

"Here," he growled, handing the sheaf of notes to her. "Five hundred."

She stared.

"Here's your bank. Get you out of vagrancy. Eight percent all right?"

That idiot Toole was smirking.

"I don't understand. . . ."

"Your bank, your bank. Don't gamblin' women have brains?"

"More than you," she snapped. "Why do men—"

The justice of the peace had collapsed into laughter. He quaked and roared up there, wheezing and hooting and wobbling, his white jowls flapping like duck wings.

"Oh," she said, unable to close the floodgates. "Oh, oh. I'm so . . . Oh."

She found her blurred way up some wooden steps, circled around the bench, and caught the old man in her arms, squeezing fiercely.

"Toole!" he bawled. "Why don't you pinch her more often?"

The image that bobbed through Amos Howitzer's telescoping spyglass startled him. Hard to tell. He focused the long tube again, twisting slightly. Those lace curtains blurred and veiled the sight, making him unsure.

He stood on the roof of The Buffalo Hump Celebrity Hall, peering into various lit windows. He did that often. No one ever spotted him up there at night, but it gave him a furtive view of the whole West End. Behind the false front the low-pitched roof raked back a hundred feet to an outdoor staircase Peach had built for just such purposes. From this vantage point Howitzer could see most of Peach's saloons and clubs, stretching up and down Park and Main Streets. Light the color of straw spilled out from them, illumining knots of soldiers, the blue of their shirts stained black by night; horses of all descriptions slouching at rails, usually with a rear leg cocked. And the drovers, who seemed to wander from saloon to saloon in twos and threes, looking like brown Indians in the coppery light. None of them ever stared up into the black bowl above; none ever discovered Howitzer at his post there.

But this night they didn't interest Amos Howitzer. Two doors south and over on Sixth, just north of the parlor houses, stood The Stockman, well lit and drawing its usual heavy trade. From his perch he'd often glassed the second-story window of The Stockman, which opened into Kate Dubois's parlor. By day he couldn't see in. The glare of sunlight, the reflection of the glass, and the lace curtains prevented it. By night the parlor usually lay dark, because Kate operated her faro layout down in the club room.

As she was doing now. Somehow the woman had gotten a bank. She'd reopened the club room with two games, both faro. Low maximums, two dollars a wager, which meant her bank couldn't stand much losing, but she'd opened nonetheless. He'd found out about that a couple of days ago. Voroshlikov over there tried to keep Peach's people out, but Jubal employed a few rannies they didn't know about and the information came easily. Miss Kate had returned to her game. And her beautiful face, with the black choker and cameo at her neck, was drawing the usual hordes of players and gazers.

It puzzled him, that bank. She hadn't gotten it from the merchants in town. He'd quietly threatened them all, told them they'd be slit from ear to ear if they banked her or bought in. This new bank would be something to find out about, he thought. Something to remedy. Somewhere, a doomed man lived. Whoever had shelled out hard money to Kate Dubois would soon be floating down the Yellowstone River.

But that wasn't what absorbed him tonight. There'd been lamplight in Kate's second-story parlor the last two or three nights, and he'd gotten curious about it. He always took his own sweet time about things, no matter what Peach demanded of him. Safer that way. Peach wanted action, any kind of action, as long as it couldn't be traced back to the Buffalo Hump and Peach himself. Amos Howitzer felt even more cautious than that. He knew intuitively that if Kate were found dead, every drover in the Territory would mob into the Buffalo Hump, drag himself, Peach, and other known employees out into the night and string them all up, proof or no proof. If not the cowboys then the swaddies, the soldiers. And if not the soldiers, he supposed the gandy dancers and railmen would try it. No. The thing required care.

But that wasn't what caught his attention. Someone in skirts walked around that parlor now and again. Not the old fat servant woman, but thin, younger, and either gray-haired or blond. The lace veiled her like gauze. The woman stirred again, crossing the room in the amber light of a single lamp, and this time his spyglass caught her. He squinted hard, pleased at his discovery, and smacked it shut. He'd have news for Peach. There'd be a reward in it. They all thought she'd skipped, caught a freight, bribed a brakeman and rode out in a rattling caboose. But there she was. Of course. In the one place she figured Peach would never catch her.

Peach had gone half-crazy at first, for want of Williams' New England Cough Remedy. Even crazier when Toole refused to give him much laudanum. But the boss had found a little among the parlor house girls and bought it, paying dearly because they knew. They always knew. Those amazons knew everything. It was an everlasting mystery to Howitzer how girls who rarely got outside knew so much.

He pocketed his spyglass and trotted off into the blackness at the rear of the Buffalo Hump. A few moments later he worked toward the front of the emerald-and-cream gaming room, which seemed half-empty again because Kate's place was roaring, and nodded to Peach. The gambler stood, ducked some amber-colored flypaper hanging from the double lamp, turned the game over to his pocked old case-keeper, Frank Ernst, shifted his unlit Cub cigar again, and walked back to his private office. Howitzer followed behind, discreetly.

Jubal Peach didn't bother with a lamp, letting the dim glow from the open door suffice. He wheeled around his small dun desk and settled himself into his quilted harness-leather chair there. "What?" he asked softly.

"I found her."

"The woman?"

"Her. She didn't leave after all."

"Where?"

"Just where you'd guess, if you thought it out."

"Don't play games, Howitzer. I have no idea."

"Kate's apartment."

Peach shifted his cigar back and forth, thinking. "Anna's dead," he said. "Get my bottles first. It's still a week before I get some from Hartford."

"She'll have used up some."

Peach glared at him. "The faster you work, the more'll be left."

Howitzer waited. If he waited, Peach usually talked. Peach couldn't stand long gaps in the talk. Silences made him nervous.

"Touchy business," Peach muttered.

"Yes."

"Might get ourselves into a jackpot. Not with Toole—he's no problem."

Howitzer sat quietly. It paid to wait. Eventually Peach would ask him. Howitzer had learned long ago not to make suggestions. Unwanted advice turned Jubal Peach into a pillar of ice. And caused trouble. So Amos Howitzer settled back in the dark, waiting.

Peach slid a hand into his natty, velvet-collared gray frock coat and pulled out the square bottle, which glinted sepia in the low light. He popped the cork, removed his unlit stogie, and sucked quietly.

"Think better with medicine," he said, jamming in the cork.

Howitzer waited silently.

"You got any ideas?"

That's how it worked. Jubal Peach would listen now. "Yeah," he said. "Let's start with what we shouldn't do."

"Torch it," said Peach. "No torch."

"Not the way the wind blows around here," Howitzer agreed. "Lookee here, Jubal. I won't run down the list. The best is a snatch. Get them women. Both. Anna and Miss Kate. Snatch them out. Sell them in some big place, Denver City, Cheyenne, San Francisco. Kate, she'll fetch a lot of money."

"They get away, they talk too much," said Peach.

"No, them sold women never talk again. First off, you

snatch away their clothes. Then you beat 'em for lessons and threaten to cut 'em up. Then you dope 'em, get 'em needing it bad. Then you keep 'em locked and doing stuff. You know. Stuff. Things they don't forget. After that, they don't talk.''

"And how'll you snatch them?"

"I got ways."

"Toole's got the telegraph. The railroad dicks. The federal marshals. The yard masters at the Diamond R and those outfits."

Howitzer smiled benignly.

Peach did too, peering into the gloom. "Anaway, that's one idea. I don't like it. I don't want the woman telling tales. I don't want trouble. I don't want these merchants making posses or going vigilante on me. I don't want all those cowboys out there saying, 'Jubal Peach did it, made Miss Kate disappear, string him up!' They'll call it murder even if they got no bodies. What else are you thinking of? Eh?''

Amos Howitzer had a way of analyzing everything. People had assets and liabilities. Kate Dubois had an asset. When you knew the asset, you always knew what to go for.

"Her face," he said.

Chapter 10

Kate's bank had fattened astonishingly. In a week she had six hundred in her upstairs safe, even after paying expenses and squaring her debt with Jubal Peach. In two weeks she had nine hundred in her bank and had opened a monte and black-jack table, each with a low ceiling. She discovered an odd thing: Some of her customers, the cowboys in particular, seemed to want to lose. Those laughing knights of the prairie flocked in, bought chips shyly, and quit while they were down ten or twenty dollars, all the while gazing raptly at her. Even the swaddies, as they called the soldiers in Miles. Usually those fellows played their thirteen-dollar monthly wage hard—but now they smiled and lost.

In the third week her bank fattened again when Elroy Duncie, who advertised himself as "capillary manipulator, boss barber, and hair dresser" over on East Main Street, dropped two hundred thirty dollars at faro, coppering the ace all night. Busted at last, he asked whether he could kiss her cheek. She smiled and offered it to him, and the lingering smack told her of hunger and yearning and maybe even courtly love. That put her bank over eleven hundred. The saloon had prospered, too, with unusual numbers of bullwhackers, hide-hunters, swaddies, and river men plunking down a dime for a mug of Bullard's or two bits for a Pink's Ginger Beer. She started ordering three barrels a day from the Bullard Brewery, at four dollars a quarter keg, plus barrel and bottle whiskey, such as Crab Orchard, Wilken Family, and Virginia Club, from eastern suppliers.

Soon she could repay Pericles Shaw, she thought. She wanted a bank of at least five hundred per game, even with low maximum bets, and she was edging toward that margin daily. The county fathers had decided to license the board games and she'd paid thirty dollars for her three, knowing Peach would pay far more for the dozens he ran. The city had decided to hire a marshal, too, and she was glad of it. It meant more protection for her—unless the city marshal turned out to be Peach's man. It worried her. Peach had been so quiet these weeks since he'd busted her that she thought he might have given up his ambition to run the whole West End.

Still she resolved to talk to Sheriff Toole about that marshal. A constable owned by Peach could hurt her trade in a hundred ways. She had another thing to talk to Toole about: Anna Waldevsky. The woman hadn't left, and seemed less inclined to go with each passing day. What had started as a favor to Sheriff Toole had become an annoyance. Anna Waldevsky had settled in upstairs, dosing herself heavily with Williams' New England Cough Remedy, scarcely bothering to dress, complaining to Lulu about whatever there was to complain about—her lumpy cot, the heat, the cold, the food, her health, boredom, the ungainly Eclipse charcoal iron, Miles City—but doing nothing at all about leaving. The addicted woman disgusted her.

That cool afternoon Kate donned the indigo brilliantine suit that complemented her hair so well and walked over to Pleasant Street, where Dr. Toole's calcimined cottage stood. She needed to talk to him. Mrs. Toole answered the door, her eyes hard. Kate had grown used to that. Every wife in town considered her a menace, and most of them considered her a low-life as well. As well they might, since The Stockman stood smack against Parlor House Row.

"I need to see Dr. Toole."

"Are you ill?"

"No. It's about other—It's about Anna Waldevsky."

The breed woman let her in, and seated her. "He's back in the barn currying Mick."

A minute later he stood in the door, his eyes roving over her and his taut face melting, the way men's faces always did when they beheld her. She'd almost grown used to it, but not quite. Why did men become enraptured over something as simple as the plane of a cheek, the size of a bosom, the spacing between the eyes, the slenderness of a nose, the softness of lips? She didn't understand it, but she knew it aroused something feral in them, some impulsive yearning that seemed to ease her own way through life, except for those embarrassing moments when men proposed out of the blue, or grew envious or jealous, or sent her gifts too extravagant and bound up with strings.

"You're as handsome as ever, lass," he said, seating her next to a shelf of *materia medica* in green tins.

Mimi Toole hovered darkly just behind him, looking dour.

"I've come about Anna Waldevsky. Peach's woman. She's still in my apartment and I can't get her to leave. Lulu's fed up with her."

"Moved in, eh?"

"Yes. She's gone through half that opiate. She scarcely bothers to dress. She complains. She refuses to go. I've asked—I've even offered to get her ticket. But—nothing. She . . . I want her out, and I'd just as soon do it decently, not turn her into the streets for Peach to capture and torment again."

"Addicts do that," he said. "Turn into vegetables. It's safe for her to go. I met the trains for days after, even the eastbound freights with nothing but rattling deadheads, and never saw any of Peach's men lounging around. The stages, too. I made a point of hanging around the Kinnear office, and the Diamond R yards. I think Peach gave up. He thinks she's gone."

"I'm sick of the woman. I don't even enjoy the privacy of my own home."

"Is she well? Eating?"

"Sick. She hardly eats. She looks . . . Her flesh is gray."

"What does she say about leaving?"

"Sometimes she says she'll go. Sometimes she just stares when I ask. Yesterday she said she missed Jubal."

"How long will her opiate last?"

"Two weeks, I think. She finished one carton. She's two or three bottles into the other. The more she drinks that stuff, the more she talks about going back to Jubal."

"She's nearing the end. If she goes back to her parents in Kansas City, she might not be able to buy bottles. So it's Jubal again."

Kate nodded. "I think it is. She wanted to get out of town right away when she first came. Now she doesn't want to."

The doctor shook his head. "Return to Jubal Peach," he muttered. "Holy Mary."

"He wouldn't give her a spoonful. He'd let her scream."

Toole nodded. "I don't know what's kept her from packing her bag and walking back to Palmer Street."

"I don't know and don't care. I wish she would. It's no joy, coping with people like that. Addicts. Drunks. I have Boris throw them out—they always make trouble. And I've told my barmen to stop serving drunks. But now I'm stuck."

She glared accusingly at him, reminding him exactly how she'd gotten stuck.

Toole smiled, his tanned face filled with amusement. "I got you into this jackpot, so I'd better get you out. Let's put her on that train. She's got family back there. Let them deal with it. If she's still got that money, have your man buy a coach seat on tomorrow's eastbound. She's supposedly going to Kansas City. Which means she'll transfer at Fargo, I suppose. Then get her to the station tomorrow. You may need help from Boris. Maybe even a hooded trap from the livery barn, if she's worried about being seen that three-block walk. Or disguise her. Dye her hair. Find a wig. Bleach it. Henna it. Find her a dress that Peach's never seen. Make her look like a parlor house woman. Whatever it takes, Miss Dubois. I'll be there at noon. At the station. Just to make sure there's no trouble."

"I'll do it—if I can get her dressed."

"Your maid strikes me as a woman who could handle that."

Kate smiled. Thanks to Boris, Lulu had mastered some exotic martial arts.

"I hear there's going to be a town marshal."

"It'll be a relief for me," Toole replied. "My practice is growing so much I don't have time to do the sheriffing any more. When I started Milestown had a few hundred people in log houses and soddies, and I hardly earned enough to stay alive. Now look at the town! It needs a marshal. County needs a real sheriff, too. And a full-time deputy. And a turn-key at the jail. I'll be pleased to give it up when my term expires. Go back to medicine. I live for the day."

He wasn't getting the drift of her concern, she thought. "Dr. Toole—has Jubal Peach had any say in getting a town marshal?"

"Holy Mary, that's what's bothering you, lass." He frowned. "I don't know. I guess I'd better find out."

"You understand why."

He nodded. "If Peach names his own marshal, he'll get you yet."

"At the clubs they're saying Peach is behind it."

Toole nodded. "I'll ask around. Horton Gatz should know something. Sylvane Tobias, too."

"If it's the wrong marshal, Sheriff, I—I'll be harassed until I shut down. Just the way I was before. Remember when Peach had a dozen bullies threatening my customers? And what you did to stop it? Suppose a city marshal just lets them do it?"

"I'll still be here."

"I know. It's just that—"

"It's all speculation, Miss Dubois. All 'What if?'. What if this marshal is Peach's bullyboy? Let's look into it."

"I can fight back. I warned Peach once. He didn't believe me. I can hire trouble of my own. I can do better than that. If I said the word, most of the cowboys in the county would go to the Buffalo Hump spoiling to tear it up. Most of the swaddies, too. They love to fight. Maybe they'd pound on Peach. Maybe I'll just show him. . . ."

Toole smiled. "You're safer than you think, Miss Dubois. Your customers aren't just customers—they're worshipers."

The thought filled her with uneasiness. "I'd better go. I'll have her at the station tomorrow. For the twelve-forty eastbound."

"I'll be there."

The man battering the door turned out to be a cowboy, his face stained nutmeg-brown by outdoor living, his blue cambray shirt bleached almost white, a plug of Dixie Kid in its pocket, and cracked muddy boots poking out below battered batwing chaps.

"You Doc Toole?"

Santiago nodded. This one had cold gray eyes; a hard look, he thought.

"I'm with the D-Cross outfit. Up from Carrizo Springs. That's Texas. We got a man injured."

"Where are you?"

"Eight miles up the Tongue."

"An emergency? What kind of injury?"

"Bullet wounds. Two."

"Where?"

"Down there at the first of them oxbows."

"No, I mean where are the bullet wounds?"

"One's through here"—he pointed at his upper left arm. "Busted that bone in there. Other's here"—he pointed just below the sternum, well to the left.

"Lost blood?"

"Some. He's pretty pale."

"How'd this happen?"

"Shot come down from that bluff. We don't know. Injun maybe."

"I'll be right along. I have a patient, but I'll let her go for now. I'll harness my buggy and meet you out front."

"Doc, the trail boss, he says I should run some errands

while I'm here. Wants me to get a credit letter to The Stock-men's and Drovers' Bank and such.''

"You don't sound southern. What's your name?''

The man grinned. "You don't sound yank, Doc.''

Santiago sighed. "All right. I'd prefer that you come, though. Which bank of the Tongue?''

"West bank. Better grass.''

"Who do I ask for?''

"Trail boss named Bolivar. Injured's handle is Short-grass.''

"All right then. It'll be over two hours.''

"Yeah. Thanks,'' the man said, and wheeled off. Santiago watched him climb aboard a gaunt, dun lineback, cow pony and swing west. He turned to his buxom, jet-haired patient, American Rose.

"I have an emergency. Irrigate with this permanganate of potash morning and evening and don't do any business for two weeks. You'll spread it and it'll come back to you. Mrs. Toole will see you out.''

"Jeez, I get up early to see you and you ditch me,'' she said.

Santiago glanced at his clock. Eleven-thirty.

He hurried out to the stable, threw harness over Mick, buckled the surcingle, slid the bit between Mick's teeth, backed the big gray between the shafts, and hooked up. Then he raced back into the house to get his surgical case. Might have to do a wagon-bed surgery, he thought, grabbing spare carbolic and sterile cloths. And oh yes, mosquito netting. He checked his Gladstone for bandaging, antiseptics, ether, and anodynes.

He remembered the last time he'd been summoned by a trail crew. Three men shot and the wounds festering, full of maggots because they'd never heard of sanitation. He put Mick into a smart trot and wheeled down Eighth to Main, and then west. He boomed across the wooden military bridge to the west bank of the Tongue, and cut south on the wagon road there. It was that time of year, he thought. Late summer, early fall, when the Texas herds began to pull in. Herds that had started in March or April down there. Several every year, spreading out upon endless empty Montana prairie, with white buffalo bones scattered across it.

A sharp wind whipped from the north, pushing his buggy south and driving Mick before it. He'd make good time, he thought. Maybe help the man, Shortgrass, if he was still alive. Shot. He'd have to look into that, too. Unusual. Starving Indians out that way, but they begged. They didn't have rifles, anyway. He'd have to comb those bluffs, looking for cartridges, whatever he could find. It smelled like a crime he'd never solve. Those drovers were a closemouthed lot, too. Probably one shot another. He'd look for powder burns.

He felt the black buggy sway under him. Usually Mick avoided work outbound, but the cold wind had whipped the barn-sour out of him. He wrapped the lines around the whip socket and pulled out a book, *Ballads and Other Poems* by Tennyson. A good poet, but full of death. That's when he got his reading done, on the buggy trips out to some remote place that meant hours of dull trotting. Except when it blew or froze or snowed or pelted him with hail, and he had to huddle under a buffalo robe and pay attention. But soon he set it aside. The dun, dry hills gripped him in a deepening melancholy. He'd come here to escape the vision of verdant Kilkenny that lurked in him, but the dun hills failed in their duty and he found himself yearning for home.

He studied the still, empty land, focusing on a distant soaring crow and the occasional silver thread of the Tongue, winding in great bows through a blistered, bronze country. The prairie stretched forever and yet seemed hollow and sere, unfit for human habitation, the preserve of mule deer and pronghorn and wolf. Gray reefs of cloud scudded south over him, and wind bit the dry grass and bent it, shook the sagebrush until it shimmered in lavender autumnal light.

He slipped the Tennyson back into the yellow oilcloth sack under the seat and withdrew instead his black, pigskin-bound missal. It was in him to ask for help. Ahead, some unknown drover lay in mortal anguish. Often on these missions of succor Santiago grew keenly aware of his own helplessness.

They expected him to help; expected a medical doctor to perform ritual magic upon the sick and wounded, and often he had no magic of his own, nothing he had learned from years of brutal study at Edinburgh, nothing but a sense of the divine, the bursting love shed upon all men. Somewhere ahead lay such a one, alive or dead. He flipped through tissued pages, finding the prayers for the sick.

"O God," he read aloud, "who by the might of thy command canst drive away from men's bodies all sickness and infirmity: be present in thy goodness with this thy servant, that his weakness being banished, and his health restored, he may live to glorify thy Holy Name. Through Jesus Christ Our Lord, Amen."

Thus he continued for a while, while Mick trotted forward along the rough road south. Done at last, he slipped the black missal back into its waterproof wrapping under the quilted-leather seat and watched the hills wind by. Some darkness gripped him. He turned idly to his memories: settling here in the wilderness to immerse himself in living death; finding and rescuing Mimi from fevers, and enjoying her unexpected love; the sheriff job. They'd come to him in 1879 after the elected man had quit suddenly. Those town fathers, such as they were. Would Santiago serve, wear the star, keep some order, until they could get a regular sheriff? He would. The office paid seventy-five a month plus some expenses. His medical practice had been netting him around twenty, plus a few chickens, vegetables, saddles, and paraphernalia. He took it, and surprised both himself and rowdy Milestown: curbing drunks, subduing brawls, once or twice nabbing dangerous outlaws. The mick doc had a few sheriff tricks in him and it surprised them, but not him. As a lad he'd brawled from one end of Kilkenny to the other.

In 1880 he'd stood for office on what they called the Irish Ticket, with men of both parties flocking to him. And had become a regular sheriff after all. But now . . . he'd fallen into a prison of his own making. His practice had grown with Miles, keeping him busy, cheating his sheriff time, cheating the public that paid him. It had to end. He'd resign soon.

There were men galore, tough and incorruptible, who'd make a fine sheriff.

He'd do that, he thought. He didn't need it anymore, and it had always been something alien to him. He'd taken life, wounded others, and it ran hard against his medical instincts. He'd been trained to heal, to save life, to knit what was broken. Now it had trapped him. He'd tell Mimi and give the county a month's notice. The thought comforted him a little. Doctor and sheriff warred inside of him, and he'd grown weary of the fight. He'd be a doctor, for there his heart and soul lay, and there he found gladness in every small thing he did for the suffering. He didn't suppose himself a very good doctor, but it had become his life, and he never stopped learning and wrestling with the small, silent enemies that felled mortals.

He rolled up a steep grade, expecting to find the herd and the wagons and Texas cowmen on the other side, where there's be a view down the Tongue for a good ten miles. Mick climbed it slowly, wearied at last by his snappy trot outbound. At the top Santiago reined in, studying the dun land that broke in rough benches off to the south. Nothing. No sign of a herd. No dust, no wagons, no men, no massed dark dots of a trail herd. Only the lines of gray cloud racing away, and the wind bending the land.

He pulled on the plaited leather fob of his chased silver Keystone pocket watch, a gift from Mimi, and read the hands: two forty-five. He'd come more than eight miles.

Then he knew. Hollowly, he snapped the watch over back and slid it into his watch pocket. He'd expected something like this all along. Someday, he'd be called out on a medical emergency that didn't exist, to remove a sheriff from the scene of a crime. He'd always lived with that, and now it had happened. He wondered briefly how they'd found out, and then knew. They'd seen old Boris buy the ticket east. Or maybe got a tip from the station men. They knew she'd catch the next eastbound. They knew how to draw Sheriff Toole far, far away. His hot Irish temper boiled.

He wondered whether Boris had been injured, or any of

the others, including Kate Dubois. But even more he wondered if Anna Waldevsky was alive or dead, free or a prisoner. He turned Mick into a loop, bumping over dry prairie, and felt the sharp, bitter wind down from Miles.

Chapter 11

Jubal sat in the brown gloom of his parlor, puffing his five-cent Eventual cigar and staring at the woman. She'd hennaed her hair, and it looked oddly right on her. But her flesh looked gray and her eyeballs yellow. Beside her Amos Howitzer stood like a meaty bulldog, his bowler askew.

"Welcome home, Anna."

"You've kidnapped me."

"Not really. You were coming back anaway."

Her gaze left his and she studied the carpet roses.

"I thought so," he added. He turned to Howitzer. "Any embarrassments?"

"No. Old Boris drove her to the station. They sat in his trap until they heard the train. She got out and walked around the station to the track. I nabbed her there, kept her in the baggage room until it left, out of his view. Train pulled out and he drove off."

Peach nodded, pleased. That was the best way.

"I'm glad to be back, Jubal."

He puffed, studying her. "You're glad to have more bottles," he said. "Let's see that bag."

Reluctantly, she handed it to him. He pawed through it, spilling her spare dress, linens, things. At the bottom lay the white cardboard carton. Eight left.

"A binge, woman. Not very thoughtful, hogging it all."

"I didn't mean to. I just—"

"What am I going to do with you?"

She looked frightened, as he intended.

"Take me back, Jubal. I'll be good to you."

"As long as I give you bottles. What if I don't?"

Her face screwed into something that looked like terror. He smiled lazily. "You've got to behave."

"I'll do anything."

"I know you will. You'll be Queen of Miles City."

She looked uncertain. "What are you going to do?"

"Teach you about love, woman."

"Don't, Mr. Peach. Let me have—"

"Tut," he whispered.

"I can't stand it without—"

"Here." He handed her an unopened bottle. She took it, staring, a tremor in her hand.

"I thought you were going to . . . you know."

"Anna. You're the light of my life. I thought I could have you forever if I . . . gave you my vice. It didn't work that way. You ran away."

She stared.

"We're both slaves, you and me. I can't throw it off, and you can't either. Maybe we'd do better sharing our slavery."

She eyed him distrustfully. "Why are you saying this?"

He puffed, letting the pungent blue smoke filter through his suit. "I could say 'Misery loves company' and you'd be content with that. But no. Anna . . . I got to walkin' the widow's walk up on top of the house, walkin' half the night after I closed up. While you were staying over there in Kate's place. I got to lookin' down over the West End, seein' my clubs, owning it all, feelin' my oats. I own Miles, almost. And no one to share it with. You gone. Me, thinkin' of the first weeks, when I was just sippin' a little stuff and you didn't know a thing of it. I got to thinkin' of that, and the good times. You're a born sport. But then that stuff got me, captured me, and I thought you'd cut loose of me because you saw how it got me, so I got you suckin' it, too. I thought maybe we could have a try together now."

Her eyes turned misty. She'd startled visibly when he'd called her by her proper name.

"You can go if you want. Catch the next train some-wheres."

She seemed bewildered. "You're not . . . I can go?"

"When you left, I thought I'd fix you some way. Make you a prisoner. Worse, maybe. But I changed my mind. Go or stay, Anna. Voluntary. That ticket's good and I'll give you a couple bottles more if you want."

"I'll stay, Jubal. I was coming home anyway. I'm so tired."

"You should eat better."

She gathered her things from the floor and stuffed them into her reticule. "I'll put these away and take a nap, Jubal."

He nodded, sucking on the cigar.

She crabbed backwards, disbelief still written on her. At the stairwell she fled upward, her feet scuffing the stair-runner.

"You surprise me some," said Howitzer.

"I surprised myself."

"You playing some kind of game with her?"

Jubal shook his head. "When she left with my bottles I was going to kill her. I've never killed anyone. I saw too much of it when the Yankees came through. . . . Anaway, I thought to take her back and make up to her."

"I didn't figure I was playing Cupid at the station."

"Did it really go that well? No hitches?"

"Perfect. They don't know she's here. Toole off and gone. No sign of him and there won't be for hours. We sent him on a long drive."

"Kidnapping's a crime, Howitzer."

"Don't see that she's been napped. She sounded eager to be back," Howitzer said. "She just needed a little push."

"A crime nonetheless. Sheriff Toole would have pinched you. Put you behind his bars. Brought you before Pericles T. Shaw."

"He got me in the knee. He's a powder puff, but he knows tricks."

"That's not the point, Howitzer."

The compact bulldog pulled out a packet of Horse Shoe

Snuff, pinched a bit into his palm, and sucked it up his nostrils. "You're working on a town marshal?" he asked.

"A delicate matter. We can't wait that long, anaway."

"What'll Toole do when he gets back?"

"Stop at The Stockman and find nothing wrong. Hunt down that cowboy of yours in every saloon in town. Talk to ticket men and baggage men. Come to the Buffalo Hump to talk with me, all squint-eyed."

"Baggage man saw us."

"Does it make any difference?"

"I don't suppose. You want me to keep an eye on him?"

"That would be helpful, Howitzer."

"Toole's gonna be mad. He'll blame us."

Jubal Peach shrugged. "I'll bring Toole over here at once and let him interview her."

He stood, signaling his wish to be alone. "I'll be at the club in an hour or so."

Howitzer let himself out. The bright daylight pierced Jubal's cranium, making him wince. But then dark enfolded him again.

He settled into his quilted chair, unsure of the next step. Lots of bottles. He'd locked his new supply, expressed from Hartford, in his office safe, hidden two bottles in a box of Cub cigars, and poured a spare into an empty Thedford's Velio Syrup bottle. These new ones he'd stow here, soon as he found a foolproof place for them. He still wanted to dole them out to her, but maybe slow her down some. She'd been awash in the stuff for weeks. Now that he had her back, he wasn't quite sure why he'd bothered. Or what he'd do next.

His sudden softness toward Anna had upset him. He supposed he'd driven such feelings out of his head forever, long ago. He'd come here for revenge. The Union Army had demolished his family and his livelihood; but here, bit by bit, he was snatching it all back with his braced decks and watered booze. It had been an obsession, repaying himself with interest. A good share of the Fort Keogh payroll vanished into his pockets each month.

He'd do even better if he could control the whole West

End. The town marshal hadn't been his idea, actually. The city fathers, Graham, Strevell, and the rest, had proposed it, seeing that Toole's practice was cutting into his law duties. Jubal had approved, offered to pay the salary as a civic gesture, proposed several men for the job—and had been coldly rebuffed. It worried him. Not that he'd been defeated. Whatever man they chose, Jubal intended to offer a small gift—say, a thousand a month. Gifts had their uses.

The marshal's first task would be to do something about The Stockman. Another touchy matter. Miss Kate had gotten a bank somewhere. Back in business. Booming business. Thousands of dollars that eluded him. He thought he'd broken her. She annoyed him, not only because she escaped his control, but because she'd rebuffed him. What a fine partner she'd make! But he hardly knew how to deal with her. He wasn't born dumb. If he went too far he'd discover a furious lynch mob at his door, ropes in hand. There were plenty of cottonwoods at the river park, two blocks west, that'd support a noose. All those cowboys and soldiers weren't going to let anything happen to Kate. Not to mention most of the merchants and ranchers and officers at Keogh. He had to find other means, some way to destroy the bond between that mysterious, beautiful, untouchable woman and her worshipers. Amos Howitzer had proposed one. Peach uncorked his medicine and gulped a swig. It helped him think. Anyway, it'd work, but he'd have to find a way to shift the blame.

Santiago steered Mick over the rumbling military bridge at the end of Main Street, feeling as cold and sullen as the pewter, overcast sky above him. He surprised Mick by turning north at once, to Palmer Street. A minute later he reined up before Peach's pile of imported tan brick.

Anna Waldevsky answered his hammering. It didn't surprise him at all. She looked gray, except for the orange dazzle of henna framing her face.

"I'd like to talk with you," he said curtly.

She nodded and let him in. The parlor reeked of stale

cigars and dark vices. She settled herself on the settee opposite him. He could barely see her in the brown gloom.

"You were kidnapped."

She shook her head.

"You're here against your will."

"That's not so, sheriff. I'm glad to be here. I came because I wanted to."

"Howitzer kidnapped you. Tell me what happened at the station. I want the truth." He glared.

She studied carpet roses for a moment. "He was there when the train came, yes. But . . . you see . . . everything is fine."

"Anna. Peach's holding you against your will. If you want to leave, we'll do it now. With my protection. You're free; you're not his wife. You can make your own life."

"I'm free anyway," she insisted. "He's not keeping me. See?"

She found her reticule on the marble-topped credenza and pulled out the ticket. "He wants me to keep it. He says if I go, he'll give me . . . enough for my vice."

"That's not the Jubal Peach I know."

Anna settled herself again. "He wanted me back. He says we're both trapped by our vice, so we should be trapped together. He even . . . uses my name again."

"But you were kidnapped."

She studied the purple roses. "I don't think so. I really wanted to come back."

"Tell me exactly what happened."

She did: Boris driving the trap down Sixth, past the parlor houses, past Bridge and Fort Streets, to the depot; then waiting in the trap for the train. Finding Howitzer on the other side of the station, out of Boris's view.

"Did he force you?"

She shook her head. "He led me to the baggage room."

"You were observed?"

"Of course. I wasn't resisting."

"But his hand clamped your arm."

She remained silent.

He fumed. "I was called out on a medical emergency. A fraud. Whoever called me out knew exactly how to get rid of Sheriff Toole for a while. A doctor answers every call. And while I was gone the train came and you were prevented from—"

"Not prevented. Jubal wouldn't do that." She waved the ticket at him.

"You gave up your liberty for a bottle."

"Are you done? I'll see you to the door."

He stood, seeing resolution in her where none had existed before.

He wasn't done. "You tell Peach that calling me out . . . calling me on a fake. . . . No, I'll tell him myself. And if I can find that fake cowboy I'll throw him behind bars so fast, he'll wonder what hit him."

He stalked out furiously, slamming the heavy door.

Home could wait. He steered his protesting dray down Sixth to The Stockman and parked it there. It had opened for the supper-hour trade. They called it supper here, instead of dinner. He found Boris pulling muslin covers off the gaming tables.

"You drove Anna Waldevsky to the train today."

Voroshlikov looked up, puzzled at the harsh tone. "I did," he said gravely. "I put her on."

"You thought you put her on. She's at Peach's."

The old man stared.

"Howitzer was waiting on the other side of the station from where you'd parked your trap."

"How'd they know?" Boris asked, puzzled.

"You bought a ticket a few days ago. Peach pays well for information."

The old man nodded. "I should have had her buy one from the conductor," he said. "Is Miss Waldevsky a prisoner?"

"She says not."

"Then you can't do anything. There's been no crime."

"I was called out of town on an emergency. That's crime enough for me. A cowboy."

He described the man, remembering the packet of Dixie

Kid cut plug in his shirt pocket. "If you see him in here send for me, Boris."

"At once. I'm sorry, Sheriff. I should have been more wary. Jubal Peach has his ways."

Out on the street, in the fading light, Santiago debated whether to go home or to stop at the Buffalo Hump. He chose the saloon, for the Irish still boiled in him. He turned the irritable Mick around the block and pulled up near the corner of Main and Park.

Peach sat there, slumped behind his faro layout as usual, shifting an unlit five-cent stogie from one side of his puffy mouth to the other.

"You've seen Anna," he said, surprising Toole. "She's happy to be home. Right?"

"With a little push from Howitzer."

"What does it matter? She's happy. You want to play?" He rapped a knuckle on the green oilcloth.

"No. Who's the cowboy?"

"You look a little put out, Doc. Maybe you should resign the sheriff job and go back to medicine. That was a long buggy ride this afternoon."

Peach wasn't even bothering to conceal it, Santiago thought. "I want that cowboy," he said.

"Any laws against summoning a doctor?"

"There are laws against obstructing justice."

Peach rapped the oilcloth again. "You'd better lose a little at my game, Toole. You're a good loser. He's over there at the far end of the bar. Right in front of your nose."

Santiago stared. The cowboy lacked chaps now. He didn't have a broad-brimmed hat on, or high-heeled boots either. His hard, lean frame was encased in a checkered suit and a collarless white shirt. He sat quietly, a mug of draft beer golden on the bar before him. Santiago knew the type. A fighter. A brass-knuckle man.

His pulse raced. He was the one, all right. The one who'd sent him on a sixteen- or seventeen-mile goose chase. The man outweighed him by fifty pounds and could outreach him, too. But Santiago had dealt with that before. Not recently.

Not even since he'd started his practice. But back in those golden wild days when he'd busted noses in Kilkenny.

The lunker watched him lazily from cool blue eyes and paused to suck an inch of beer.

"You going to pinch him?" Peach asked amiably.

No, Santiago thought, he wouldn't. He had something better in mind. He walked that way, aware that he had no weapons. He wore his medical clothing, black frock coat and pants, and wasn't even wearing his star. Which suited him fine.

"You want something, Doc?" asked the man, smiling faintly.

Santiago shoved. At the same moment he hooked the man's stool with his foot and pulled. The man toppled backward, surprise on his face, hitting an Acme Queen parlor organ behind him with a hard smack of his back and head. He kicked, jamming the stool back into Santiago.

A cool one, Toole thought, feeling the wild pulse race through him, feeling his black Irish soul up in his throat. The man rolled sideways and up, fast as an unpaid tart, and bulled forward, crouched and ready to punch. Santiago threw the beer at him, blinding him for a moment. The man slammed in, hitting Santiago hard with mean fists, once on the ear, again on his left shoulder, and again off his ribs, sending white pain lacing through him. Santiago brought the mug down hard, smacking it into the man's greased brown hair. It shattered, cutting Santiago. But the man caved slowly to the floor, knocked unconscious. Toole kicked at the man's left knee for good measure. Someone shouted.

"You don't fight fair, Toole." That was Amos Howitzer's gravelly voice.

Santiago pulled a handkerchief from a pocket and pressed it against the lacerations on his right hand, ignoring Howitzer.

"You taking him in?" Peach's voice.

Toole ignored him, knotting his handkerchief into a temporary bandage. His palm and index finger oozed blood. He felt good.

"You fight dirty, Toole. You didn't even warn him. You hit him with glass." Howitzer's voice.

The burly man on the floor groaned, coming around. He'd have a knot on his head. Maybe a concussion. Toole booted him in the ribs. The serving women squealed.

"You're disturbin' the trade, Sheriff." Peach's voice.

"That wasn't Sheriff Toole. That was Dr. Toole. Tell him that when he comes around."

Santiago walked quietly into the clean air outside and drove Mick home one-handed.

Chapter 12

The dour dressmaker hooked the last of the little buttons and stepped aside. Anna stood quietly in the center of the parlor, waiting for the verdict.

"Perfect!" said Peach. He circled around her, admiring the tightly fitted, wine-red velveteen dress, trailing blue smoke from the Hilt's Best between his lips.

"I feel naked," she said, peering down at the expanse of white flesh rising from the low-cut bodice.

"You'll get used to it. Good for the trade."

"I don't know how you can see how she looks in here," the dressmaker said.

"Sun makes me squint. And she'll be in the club at night anaway." He eyed the surly woman. "Make two more, one cream and one . . . What goes with that orange hair she's got? One green. Light green. All this same stuff."

Anna looked like she wanted to say something, but he cut her off. "Costumes for the club," he said easily. "Let me do the deciding, Anna."

She nodded unhappily.

He dismissed the woman, Mrs. Bottoms, who scurried out. Anna stood quietly while he circled her again, liking it all, kicking himself for not thinking of it sooner.

"You'll learn it fast enough. It's not brains that count but care. You take care, and you'll do fine."

"They'll be looking at my bosom."

"That's right. That's the draw. That's what you got over that Virgin Kate. That's what'll get me the trade. They'll

114

5

DEUCES AND LADIES WILD

115

come over to see Mrs. Peach, and she's no maiden. She's a
fine woman, not yet thirty, with henna hair that shines like
a conductor's lantern and white shoulders and a bit of . . . a
bit of the exotic, Anna. You'll enjoy it.''

"I'm a proper woman."

"Course you are. Who says you aren't? You're just allow-
ing a peek, a promise, that's all. Now there's things you got
to do. The Williams'. You can't be drinking that outa the
bottle now. It looks like whiskey anaway, so we'll just bring
you a glass whenever you order. I'll have the women bring
it. Looks just like a sip of Kentucky.''

"I don't know how I'll learn the game."

"Well, all you got to do is watch a few nights. The bets
are even. They win, you just pay as many chips as they got
bet."

She smiled faintly. "Maybe it'll work, Jubal."

"That's it. Smile a lot. Smile at each man that comes up.
Make each one think you're offerin' something. . . . You
know."

"It could be fun—if I ever get used to it." She found her
reticule, dug for a handkerchief in it, and stuffed it into her
décolletage. Then she pulled it out. "I guess I'll forget it.
Just so they know I'm not a parlor house woman.''

"You're Peach's wife. They know that."

"I suppose."

"Let's go then," he said. "You'll be the Queen of Miles
City tonight. It's a new era for the Peaches.''

She found a cape and wrapped it over her exposed shoulders, and they stepped out into the late-afternoon sun. He
felt pleased. The woman looked handsome. More than handsome. From the time he'd thought up the idea she'd been
half-captivated and eager. Afraid too, but mostly eager. Anna
Waldevsky was about to live the life she'd dreamed of when
she ran away with him. And just maybe she'd snatch back
Kate Dubois's trade. Good idea anaway, having a pretty gal
dealing.

He'd start her square. Teach her the edge later. Let her
play square for a while now; let the trade come in, play, win

a little. Let her get a reputation, let the cowboys and soldiers tell themselves they could win at Anna Peach's table. In a month or two he'd show her the edge and then he'd really rake it in.

She thought she'd be too dumb, and Peach wondered about it. But he had plenty of dumb dealers. All it took was care and checking. Look at the bets. Look at the cards. Do it right. Soda to hock. Twenty-five turns and start over. Pay the exact amount, chip for chip, same color, same value. Watch for the coppered bet.

"You'll do fine, Anna," he said as they walked east on Palmer.

"I forgot my Cough Remedy," she said, panicked.

"Lots at the club."

"I have to get it."

He caught her arm. "Come on to the club. We get in, I'll get you a bottle. In my office we'll pour it into a Old Quaker rye bottle I got."

"Don't torture me, Jubal."

She didn't trust him, but she came along. He'd get her the juice fast. He slid an arm about her slim waist, steering her possessively down Park toward Main. She smiled at him.

"I feel naked," she said, and giggled.

The Buffalo Hump Celebrity Hall was off and running when they got there, barmen waiting for the evening trade, lamps lit and smoking a bit, the cream-and-green enamels shining in warm light. He steered her back to his office, opened his safe, extracted a bottle of the Williams', and poured it all into the rye bottle. All before her eyes.

"We'll leave this at the bar. I'll tell the women. You order rye, they'll bring you this."

The evening went splendidly, Anna sitting beside him while he dealt faro, cowboys and railroad men gathering, eyeing her white chest and peeping breasts, and sitting down to lose some coin. She studied the game attentively, mastering it. By ten he had more players than his table could handle, and they began to spill to the other games. All because Anna drew them. Word ran up and down the West End, and they came.

At eleven she wanted to go home, but he urged her to hang on. Her eyes had bagged and she'd sucked too much of the thick amber syrup that passed for rye. At midnight he let her go. Howitzer took her home. She would need to get her sleeping time worked around until she could stay up through the night, sleep mornings. Then she'd see the value of his heavy drapes.

The next night he let her rake in the losing bets and pay the winners. She missed some of them, especially the coppered bets, and he drilled her with it. A chip with a copper token on it meant the card had been bet to lose. If the card lost, the bet won. It mystified her at first.

The third night he let her draw cards from the slot in the case box and call them, loser, winner. Let her shuffle and turn over the soda, and put the cards into the box, and put the cap with the tiger emblem back on. She attracted the trade; no doubt about it. Swaddies and gandy dancers hung around, peering at her white chest and dropping chips.

The next night he put a lookout on the ladder seat that rose just behind her.

"He can see right down my front," she complained later.

"He ain't paid for that, but it's a bonus. He's paid to watch the board. We get this many waddies and they get sneaky. They push out extra chips to winners after each turn. He's up there to stop that. You gotta watch all the time. They'll slip it to you. Work in pairs. On one side of the table one'll ask you something, and you'll be talkin' with him while the other slips chips out. The case-keeper's sposed to look too, but he's busy pushing beads. When you're playing one or two, you can keep track easy enough. It's like tonight, with a bunch standing around, they get foxy. You let the case-keeper and the lookout help. They usually signal, tap, click, rather than tell you some gent's cheatin'."

"I don't even know their names."

"You don't need to know. Call 'em all Eddie or something. They're all Eddie."

She laughed.

"You want to try it alone tomorrow?"

"You think I'm ready?"

"Sure. And if you got doubts, just ask the lookout."

"He's got a shotgun up there, Jubal."

"Keeps the peace," Jubal said. And keeps anyone from protesting very hard, he didn't say aloud.

"Make sure I got enough medicine," she muttered.

He let her take the game the next evening. She got flustered a few times and kept ordering Old Quaker, but she handled it. Handled a larger mob than any dealer enjoyed working. He stood at his bar, congratulating himself. Anna was sucking trade out of The Stockman, and if the town marshal proved to be tractable Peach'd drive out Kate for good. And no one would know he'd had a hand in it.

The hard, muscular man beside him sipped Crab Orchard and stared.

"Your head still hurt, Walden?"

Walden ran a weathered hand through brown hair, finding the lump there.

"It does. And my eyes ain't normal yet. I get tired, I see things double."

"Beer-mug concussion, Walden."

"He fights the way I fight. I didn't expect that from a doc."

"No one did. That's why the uptown people hired him. They knew something we didn't."

"I'll kill him," muttered Walden.

"You wouldn't kill a mick doctor, would you?"

"Wait and see."

"You hang on. Let me bag the town marshal first. Might save us both some embarrassment."

"When?"

"I'll know tomorrow, Walden. If I don't bag the marshal, I'll have two jobs for you. Provided you get out of town right after. You'll enjoy one, and probably dislike the other. But the price is right."

* * *

Peach lost. He didn't find out until Pike Garrison walked into the Buffalo Hump around nine that evening. Garrison stood six and a half feet in stockings, wore a luxurious black handlebar mustache, and was so thin that his muscles rose in lumps over a cadaverous frame. He wore a mackinaw against the evening chill, and on it was a star cobbled out of a silver dollar by a town smith. His weapon of choice was a sawed-off two-barrel Greener, which hung loosely in a cocked arm.

Peach watched the man from the bar, where he sipped Kentucky. Garrison stood at the batwing doors, slowly surveying the Buffalo Hump, his slate eyes studying Anna at the faro table and then settling on Jubal.

The gambler fumed. The merchants had rejected his offer. Hire Clem Walden, who knew his way around the West End and could keep the peace, he'd told them, and he'd pay Walden's entire salary. Good business, he'd added. Clem would keep peace in all the clubs, collect the gaming table license fees, saloon fees, parlor house fees, and give half to the city. Clem would pinch drunks, run undesirables out of town, keep a lid on the swaddies from Fort Keogh. Clem would share the jail office with Santiago Toole, help when Toole was out doctoring.

Only they didn't choose Walden. They chose the quietest man in Miles City. One-Word Garrison. A man with no known loyalties to anything. Peach brightened at that. The town fathers wouldn't know any more about Garrison than he did. In fact, it might work out after all.

"Evenin'," said Garrison.

"You're the new marshal. Well, that's fine. Keep the peace around here."

"Yes."

"The West End needs it. Toole's too busy. I was thinking of hiring my own security for the clubs. They get to brawling—the soldiers and the cowboys."

"Yes."

"Well, let's celebrate, Garrison. Want you to feel welcome here. Any time. Stop by for a drink, a talk. You want to know who's causing trouble, I'll tell you. I got seven clubs and all my men keep me informed. Now, what can I get you? How about a shot of Crab Orchard? Beer?''

"No."

"Well, fine. Keep fresh on the job. You must be working an evening beat. Got hours, I suppose. You'll divide with Toole. Take a load off him. Mind if I ask what the town's giving?''

"Fifty.''

"You're worth more, Garrison. Or shall I call you Pike? Worth more. That hardly buys a bunk and chow. I tell you what—here at the bar we got sandwiches, pickles, boiled eggs. You just dip in any time. Stretch a city marshal salary. We'd be pleased, a way of paying for our protection.''

Garrison remained silent, studying the club and its patrons with those opaque slate eyes. Was the man devoid of all expression, Jubal wondered? The gambler had never encountered a man whose face he was less able to read.

"How do you like the job so far?''

"So far, it's fine.''

"There's a rough element here needs watching. My barkeepers got shotguns.''

Garrison nodded.

"You take a lot of risk for a small wage,'' Peach said. "Capitalists always say the more risk, the more return they should get on the investment.''

Garrison nodded, his eyes studying Anna, who was dealing to a dozen waddies.

"You gonna keep a regular schedule? Walk your beat regular?''

"Random. Any time.''

"Well, that's fine. No one knows when to expect the marshal. Keep 'em guessing, I suppose.''

Garrison nodded, his back to the bar, his gaze penetrating every corner of The Buffalo Hump Celebrity Hall.

"You're a man to deal with, Garrison. Toole, now. Not as tough. Oh, he has some tricks and keeps the peace well enough. But he's a doc. Not a real lawman. You make me feel more secure around here.''

"Toole never failed yet.''

"He's a doc.''

Garrison's slate eyes bored into Peach's. ''Don't know that you want more law than Doc Toole gave you, Peach.''

That was a lot of words for Garrison. Jubal felt elated. ''You planning on more law?''

"Yes.''

"You know, Garrison. Too much law around here, and business drops. The waddies stay away. Wet blanket. When business drops, the whole town suffers.''

"Get the laws changed.''

"Anaway, I'm looking for more security. For all my clubs. I'm thinking, maybe you'd like some off-duty income. Do one shift for the town and do another shift private, for the clubs. I'd make it worth your while.''

Garrison eyed him attentively.

"Five hundred a month. Private shift.''

Something shrank in Garrison's slate eyes. His drooping black handlebar mustache twitched. ''Too much for the job.''

"Well, if you'd do it for less, of course I'd be delighted. How about three hundred?''

Garrison didn't say no.

"Look, man. Those aldermen don't know what it's like. I know. You go out into the night and risk a bullet. Risk getting hurt. Even some sloppy drunk'll suddenly pull a piece and shoot. Lawmen are the thin line between peace and big trouble. More so out here. Just the thin line. My thinking is, pay a man what he's really worth. A man on private shift is worth plenty.''

"No.''

Peach saw his hopes sliding away. ''You think about it. Offer's open any time. I need a man.''

"You got one over there.'' Garrison nodded toward a man on a bar stool. Walden. ''Got another back there.'' He nodded toward Amos Howitzer hovering near the office door. ''Fact is, you got five more than you need.''

Irritation boiled through Peach. He needed some Williams'. He turned to the barman. "Want some Old Quaker rye," he muttered.

Garrison watched attentively.

The syrup arrived in a short glass. Peach swilled it down. Garrison studied it.

"Good rye," Peach said, feeling better at once.

"You've got violations here."

Something cold drained through Jubal Peach.

Garrison nodded toward Anna. "She shouldn't be dealing in here. Those bar women shouldn't be here. City ordinance."

Peach gripped the mahogany bar. The Cough Remedy worked through him. "You enforcing it across the board?"

"Yes."

"At The Stockman?"

"It doesn't apply to Miss Kate, if that's what you mean."

"What do you mean?"

"You should know. You drafted it and pushed it through the council."

Peach dug around in his memory for the language. Saloonkeepers shall not employ, serve, or permit women to loiter in places where spirits are sold. Fine, ten dollars first offense, thirty thereafter.

"You going to enforce that?"

"Better have them out tomorrow."

"You going to pinch Kate Dubois?"

"City attorney and the justice—Shaw—tell me it can't apply to an owner, violates her rights. If she served or hired women I'd pinch her. She's in that separate club room, anyway."

Cold rage ran through Peach, but he bit it off. "Anna's half owner. Wife."

"Better show me partner papers. Maybe build a separate gaming room, like Kate. No women tomorrow, Peach."

The new marshal wandered out. Jubal Peach stared at his retreating back.

Howitzer waited a discreet moment and then slipped over to Jubal.

"What?" he asked.

"Braced deck," muttered Jubal. "Bad spin."

Walden joined them, curious.

"You lost, Clem. They picked Garrison. And they're moving on me."

"Nothing we can't fix."

"We got to be a little careful," Peach said. "You two made some plans for Kate. Her assets."

Howitzer nodded.

"Don't do it until the alibi is worked out. Around here, they hang people for less."

Chapter 13

Love came unbidden into the life of Amos Howitzer, interfering with his professional duties. He could not do what Jubal Peach insisted he do, and it drove him to dyspepsia. What troubled him most is that it had been his own idea. He'd recognized Kate Dubois's real asset, knew how to destroy it, and had proposed the whole idea to Peach. But once Peach had commanded it, Howitzer shied away from it and saw a thousand reasons not to proceed with it. The feeling bewildered him. He'd never before allowed the slightest sentiment to interfere with his professional duties. In fact he was proud of his cold and unsentimental nature, which permitted him to do anything necessary without attacks of remorse or gout or melancholia.

Amos Howitzer had grown up in a small burg south of Indianapolis called Shelbyville, where his family ran the Cannon brand vinegar distillery. He had that typical Hoosier combination of saccharine sentimentality and base morals, though he never admitted to a sentimental streak in him, the streak that was his undoing now. He'd run away from home after he'd dumped a fifty-pound tin of baking soda into a vinegar vat to spite his father, and had never seen Indiana again. He'd drifted west and found his true calling as a saloon man in the cattle towns of Kansas. He'd been paid well to keep the drovers up from Texas reasonably docile, and was responsible for the disappearance of several Texans in Ellsworth and Wichita.

He loved Kate Dubois from afar, and felt deprived because

he could no longer enter The Stockman and gaze upon her glowing beauty. The whole night of the big game he'd stared at her transfixed, secretly hoping she'd triumph over Peach. She reminded him of his mother, inexpressibly virtuous and tender and pure. Had Kate been the other kind of woman, such tender feelings never would have burgeoned in the breast of Amos Howitzer. But Kate plainly guarded her virtue, bestowed love upon all around her, and generally behaved as any noble Hoosier mother might.

At first he wouldn't admit it. No Hoosier ever admitted to sentimentality, even though they all oozed with it. Nonetheless, he managed to weigh his task in purely practical terms. How could he destroy her assets and yet have a perfect alibi? He considered broken beer bottles, and muriatic acid, and the work of a barlow knife. He considered kidnapping, forcible entry, various types of abduction, and other ruses. He considered wearing a Harvest Queen flour sack with holes cut for his eyes and nose; a soldier's uniform; a Ku Klux Klan costume—very convenient, he thought—and other disguises. Of all these the Klan costume would plainly serve best, and divert attention from Peach and himself.

By clandestine means he ordered the necessary raiment from Montgomery, Alabama, and soon thereafter Railroad Express delivered a large trunk containing a Grand Dragon's uniform, along with sheets for a Grand Titan, Grand Giant, Grand Cyclops, Hydras, Furies, and Ghouls. Plus a charter vesting supreme authority for the Territory of Montana in him. True, he thought, Peach was a southerner, but no one would connect the formation of a Klan Dominion with Peach the gambler. Miss Kate Dubois would simply be the victim of a Klan incident; a burning cross, a brief abduction, some facial surgery that would impose Klan insignia upon her forever.

Ah, the genius of it! His next step was to post some hand-lettered broadsides around Miles, warning that the Klan would deal with undesirables soon. That resulted in some considerable puzzlement in the northern cow town. Sheriff Toole had torn them down as fast as he'd spotted them. Which was fine with Howitzer. He wanted Toole and the new marshal, Garrison, and the town fathers to worry about the Klan. One night he'd soaked a wooden cross in coal oil and planted it in the cemetery on the grave of a Chinese. The orange flame flickered eerily over Miles City, and people watched and waited for the secret society to strike its victims.

"An alibi for sure," said Peach in the privacy of his office. "Now go do it."

"Not ready yet," Howitzer said. "If we do it right, we'll take care of Toole, Pericles Shaw, and Pike Garrison, too. All in one blow. But I have to set it up a while more."

"I can't wait. Ever since Garrison shut down Anna I've lost trade back to The Stockman. It's personal now. Anna liked it. First time since we teamed up, she's doing something she likes. And we're raking it in, too. They came to her table, Howitzer. They liked her looks. They bought chips. Now she's at home guzzling that syrup and blaming the law. And I can't get the city council to repeal the ordinance."

"Mr. Peach, there's three commandments out here, and we'd best mind them or it might be our necks. Thou shalt not steal; thou shalt not murder; and thou shalt not harm a decent woman. If we get caught, Mr. Peach, every waddie out on the prairies, every soldier who can bust loose, and every brakeman for a hundred miles will string us up and the law won't be no protection. You let me get the Klan established, and then we'll be safe enough."

Peach glared at him, hating the delay but succumbing to his logic. "Who've you got?"

"Only Walden now. I don't want word leaking out. Clem, he's going to take care of Toole and Garrison; me, I'll take on Kate. I'll need the other gents to help me get past old Boris, and that Turk in there. Don't forget Turks."

"Do it in plain sight?"

"Sure. Shank of the night. When a few dozen people see the Klan sheets. We want witnesses."

"Where?"

"We'll haul her from her faro table right out of there, take her out into the night."

"What about Toole?"

"Go get him. Kill the breed woman first, so it looks like Klan business. Then him."

"What about the rest?"

"Shaw lives alone; easy pickings. Garrison may be out on his beat. We'll keep track. Probably suck him into The Stockman where we want him."

"Why not now?"

"Too soon. Klan's got to make itself known."

Peach nodded. "It'll work," he said. "Howitzer, you're some cannon. Are all Hoosiers like you?"

"Naw, they're shiftier. Put two Hoosiers together and you've got a crime wave. Put three together and you've got a church."

But Amos Howitzer had his doubts. He could no more carve upon Kate's beautiful face than he could hamstring a thoroughbred horse. He'd gazed raptly at her for hours, at her gentle gray eyes, her ready smile, her soft blond hair tied with a yellow ribbon, the black choker and cameo at her throat, her long delicate fingers that pulled cards from the case box without guile. She'd even smiled at him before the big game, before she'd pulled the burial business on Jubal. She was like all the good sisters of the world, untouchable. The very thought of gouging her flesh, while she screamed and writhed, paralyzed him.

"Walden," he said at the bar, "you want to switch? You want to tackle her and me tackle Toole and the rest?"

"No. I don't carve up women, Howitzer."

Howitzer glanced around quickly to see if anyone had heard, but no one had. The two of them guzzled Crab Orchard alone, out of earshot.

"We got to be more careful," he muttered.

He slid out into the night and walked along Main, and then down Sixth, pausing at the lamp-lit window of The Stockman. From a certain vantage point he could see clear through the saloon and into the club room in back, to her table. He saw her there, in her usual white blouse with the puffed sleeves, dealing, her fingers occasionally pushing vagrant blond hair back from her face, smiling, virginal. . . .

He turned into the night, knowing he'd falter when the moment came and hating the sentimental streak in him. He thought of resigning and hated that, too. It'd ruin his reputation in certain circles. He felt trapped. Peach had asked too much this time, even though his own little scheme would work all too well. He could kill Kate more easily than he could carve up that exquisite face, with its fine bones and planes and fresh, creamy skin.

Her asset, he thought, along with a slim, perfect body. But there was more, he admitted. She treated each man who came to her table so sweetly, so affectionately, by first name, that they'd come even if she were less beautiful. Even if she were like . . . everyone's mother, he thought. Everyone's sister. No. Everyone's girl. They were all sweet on her. For a moment he raged at all his rivals, the hundreds of them who'd basked in her smile and her attention. He loathed them all. She belonged to him!

He saw that new town marshal wandering along, checking the clubs, and he turned south, along the silent parlor houses, trying to make sense of his plans and sentiments. He'd never felt so trapped. He thought maybe he'd go tell Peach it wouldn't work; find some practical excuse. But in fact he knew the whole Klan business would work spectacularly well, and deal with all of Peach's rivals and enemies in one blow. He thought of warning Toole, who had his grudging respect. Tell the sheriff. But he'd never been a stool pigeon and never would be. It amazed him that he even considered it. Maybe he could tip Kate. Just tip her off. She'd flee. She'd get out of Miles. She'd take the hint in a hurry. He liked that. He'd tell her if he had to. Maybe he could work for her, then. He'd wait a few more days and then tell her. She'd love him for that, maybe make him her fellow. Maybe there was something to being a Hoosier after all, he thought, rounding a corner.

* * *

Santiago watched the cross flame and roar in his front yard. Mimi, beside him, raged at it like a hissing cat. They'd been awakened by an eerie pulsing light that made their bedroom dance. He stared at it now, sensing hatred, feeling its evil. Beyond its glow neighbors collected on Pleasant Street, watching it with silent alarm, dread caught in their throats.

He felt Mimi's terror and drew her close to him.

"Why, Santo? Why?"

He hated to tell her. "We're people they don't like," he said cautiously.

"Why, Santo?"

"Southerners started it after the war. Mostly to terrorize blacks, but also others. People of color. And immigrants."

She pulled herself closer to him. The cross spat flame at them, snapping like a rabid wolf in the night.

"But you're a doctor. You've done nothing but help. . . ."

"Hatred doesn't exempt anyone, Mimi."

"But, Santo, this is the North! The West!"

"Half, maybe two thirds the people in this territory are southern, Mimi."

"Will they hurt us?"

Santiago remained silent. The answer, he knew, would be yes. Probably Mimi first; maybe himself.

"Let's go away!" she exclaimed. "I hate this place!"

He'd been thinking the same thing. But first he'd try to root it out. The posters had appeared a week earlier, handlettered, on various stocks, often cut from cardboard boxes. Warnings. Names. Threats. Demands that one or another person leave. One gave Kate Dubois twenty-four hours to leave town and alleged she lacked virtue. He'd ripped it down, angrily. Another threatened Chang Loon. Leave or die. Others had been hammered to the walls of the parlor houses that had black girls. Leave or die. Each signed by someone calling himself Grand Dragon, the Klan leader of a state or territory.

But nothing had happened, at least so far. He and Pike Garrison had doubled their watches. The new town marshal had been a blessing, taking a big load off of Santiago. Pike shared his office, took the evenings while Santiago took the mornings. But no sooner had the town hired Pike than this writhing snake coiled into Miles City, terrorizing the whole town.

He'd pursued it. Checked with every merchant in town: who'd bought ink or brush? Who'd bought cardboard, or begged boxes? Who'd made threats? He and Pike queried every saloon-keeper and barman in town. What had they heard? And they'd come up with nothing. He'd sat down and drawn up a list of southerners, former Rebs, sympathizers. It grew beyond his reckoning. Most of the drovers up from Texas had served in the Confederate Army. The sports and saloon men had come up from border states, like Missouri, or the south. During the war the Union Army had simply sent captured Rebs west. Many came. They'd tried to name the Alder Gulch digs Varina, after Jeff Davis's wife, until a yank judge stopped it and named the place Virginia City. They'd called the biggest gold strike in the territory Confederate Gulch.

The list grew so long it bewildered him and amounted to no help at all. He'd be better off putting a stool pigeon on it, or getting one of the barmen—Murphy, he supposed, a friend of his and a friend of the law—to listening and reporting back to him. He'd talk to Murphy over at The Grey Mule. That'd be a start.

"I'm afraid, Santo. This is because I'm Indian—part Indian."

"Seems there's more to it, Mimi."

Out in the dancing darkness Pike Garrison pushed through the gate in the white picket fence. He stared at the mesmerizing flame and detoured around it. He wore a gray cotton union suit, bagged at the elbows, brown corduroy britches and boots. And carried his sawed-off Greener, which glinted in the glow.

"You all right, Toole?"

"So far."

Garrison nodded. "I just got to bed." He yawned. "This is something."

"Come on in, Pike. We'll talk."

They stared at the dying cross, wondering if with the wind it might endanger Toole's cottage, and went in. Mimi lit their way to the kitchen and started to heat water.

Garrison settled in to a kitchen chair, scratching his head. "I don't know how to stop this."

"Figure out who's next, and be there," Toole suggested.

"No one's dead yet."

"I have no theory."

"I hate Rebs."

"We've got people to protect," said Santiago, wearily. "Chang Loon especially. And his family. And the five or six other Celestials. And some of those girls on Sixth Street. And Mimi."

"Maybe you, Toole."

"Likely they'll come after me."

They sat in the amber lamplight, pondering it.

"Forget evidence, Toole. What's your hunch?"

"Peach."

Garrison nodded.

"Any bunch of Texas cowboys."

"Railroad lads hate the Chinese," Garrison said. "But it don't signify."

"Nothing adds up."

"It's Peach," muttered Mimi.

"Do you know that?" Santiago asked.

"It's him."

She often had mysterious insights and he respected them. "We'll start there, I guess. He's been mean as a sore tooth since you enforced the ordinance, Pike."

Garrison shook his head. "Hardly makes sense."

The teapot whistled at last, and Mimi poured three cups.

Restlessly, Santiago stalked to his medical office and peered out. The cross had collapsed into red embers and most of his neighbors had gone back to bed. A few hovered like white ghosts out on the street, in wrappers and greatcoats and slippers, too disturbed to go home. His seven-day clock said three-fifteen.

There, in the darkness of his office, he felt fear. For himself. For Mimi. Especially for her. What if they drew him out on a medical call again? What if they struck while he walked his rounds? Or was making sick calls right in town? He felt a helplessness reach through him and turned back to the kitchen.

"Mimi," he said. "I can't protect you. Any time I'm walking rounds, or at the jail, or out on medical calls, you're alone."

"I can fight. I know how to shoot."

He nodded. "Pike can't protect you either. He sleeps mornings. And we've both got to watch Chang Loon and his family. And the girls on the line. Two of us against . . . a lot, maybe. And they've got all the advantage of surprise."

"I can do without sleep, Toole. I'll guard her." Garrison blew on the tea and sucked it noisily through his drooping mustache. "Wish I knew, though."

"Take it to Peach," she said. "Take it. Whether or not you know for sure."

"Can't rightly do that, ma'am."

"We can publish a few things of our own, Garrison. A few handbills," Toole asserted.

"That don't root out badgers."

"If this continues this town's going to blow up, some way," Toole muttered. "Lynching, mobs, you name it."

Santiago slumped wearily. He'd been trained to save lives, heal the sick. The lawing had come to him unbidden, and he'd lawed. He was sheriff. As it always had, everything was now landing on his shoulders.

"Pike," he said sharply. "This has nothing to do with Mimi. It's got nothing to do with race, either. Scaring the Chinese, the parlor house girls. It's aimed at me, Pike. It's coming roundabout, but it's aimed at me. At Sheriff Toole."

Garrison stared from hard gray eyes and said nothing.

"It's Peach," said Mimi.

"I think you're right, Mimi. You look at the people in this town, you ask who's happy, who isn't. Who's got ambitions, who doesn't. Who's frustrated, who isn't. Peach's frustrated.

We've kept Anna out of his saloon. He can't compete. The Klan's warned Kate Dubois on grounds everyone knows are false. Warned me now. He wants to drive out Kate. And he wants his own law. And he wants Anna to deal in his saloon. Maybe use other women in his other saloons. He's trying to scare her out, Pike."

Garrison stood. "Getting late. Tomorrow I'll hang around Miss Kate's bar."

"They might burn out Chang Loon, Pike."

"Can't be everywhere, Toole."

Santiago let Pike out the dark front door and gathered up a twelve-gauge. It was going to be a long, tiring night, but he had no intention of sleeping.

Chapter 14

The early days of fall slid by in a red whirl of exhaustion. Santiago pulled himself out of his warm bed well before dawn and patrolled the silent misty streets of Miles, spending a lot of time checking on the town's Chinese and his friend Chang Loon. He stalked through the small hours like a wraith, shotgun in hand, ready to strike. His eyes bagged and his head buzzed and he grew testy. He huddled in the dark dawn across from the parlor houses that had been threatened, learning more than he wanted to know about some men in town but nothing about those who made threats.

He kept up his practice as best he could, knowing a tired doctor missed things, made bad decisions. Sometimes, in moments between patients, or when he was driving his buggy to an outlying ranch, he fell asleep. Somehow Mick got him where he was going. He made a new rule for himself: No longer would he take out-of-town calls from strangers. These he would refer to the Keogh post surgeon, Adelbert Hoffmeister. He would not let himself be drawn away from Miles again. Even on calls he trusted he worried about Mimi. She caught his concern, his seriousness, and took measures of her own, staying alert for trouble on the street, locking doors, keeping a weapon at hand.

He and Pike Garrison had some broadsheets printed at *The Yellowstone Journal*, simply announcing that anyone who threatened the life, health, and civil rights of others would be prosecuted to the fullest extent of the law. Each day he nailed one of these to his sheriff's office door and sometime

134

each day or night it was torn off by parties unknown. Which let him know that the serpent was still coiled in Miles City, even if it had yet to strike.

Sometimes he patrolled through the evening with Pike Garrison, even though they'd divided up the work and nights were given to the town marshal. They both figured evening would be the time trouble would erupt, and they wanted to be ready. And on more than one occasion he bumped into Garrison, quietly backing Santiago in the pre-dawn dark. He liked the taciturn man. Perhaps with Garrison's help he could continue as sheriff without damaging his practice.

Nothing happened, and yet the town crouched like a catamount ready to strike, its long tail lashing, its prey observed by cold, unblinking eyes. Santiago felt it; felt trouble in his bones, even though the days slipped by harmlessly. He began to wonder whether he could let up, return to normal hours, get some sleep. But something in his soul resisted, something in him knew that trouble still percolated in back alleys and dark saloons.

Late afternoons he usually stopped at The Grey Mule, down on Park Street, to check with his friend Jocko Murphy, the barman there. Jubal Peach didn't own The Grey Mule, although he controlled the gambling tables, and his dealers had big ears. Murphy usually set up a foaming glass of beer and then dropped a few cryptic words. His news usually boiled down to gossip. A lot of the sports were wondering which southerners in Miles had formed a chapter of the Klan. Peach's name came up a few times. Once, Peach's man Howitzer had wandered in with one of the sheriff's broadsides in hand, and enjoyed reading it to other patrons.

One October day a woodcutter named Thorstad summoned him. There'd been an accident down at a camp fifteen miles south, where jack pine grew rank. Santiago notified Garrison he'd be gone all day, told Pericles Shaw and Sylvane Tobias to keep a sharp eye on Mimi and the rest of the potential victims in town, and drove out, letting Mick pick his way down the east-bank road along the Tongue. He tried to sleep but couldn't, and finally sunk deep into his padded seat in an angry stupor, knowing this couldn't continue much longer. He was too drained to practice good medicine, too exhausted to be a good sheriff. He'd managed to gather his surgical chest and Gladstone bag full of *materia medica*, but he'd forgotten a weapon of any sort.

The injured party turned out to be a man he knew, Cletus Gantt, a bearded giant in his forties whom Santiago had thrown in the jail more than once for drunken brawling. They led him into a crude log shack, to a wooden bunk there, and Santiago didn't like what he saw. Gantt lay unconscious, pale, ice-cold, blue, with shallow breath. He'd been sawing through a tree when it cracked like a cannon shot and whipped sideways, smashing Gantt's hip and flinging him twenty feet. Something was busted, so they'd hauled him back to the shack and summoned help.

Something busted, Santiago thought bitterly. They should have left the man alone, covered him, gotten help. Gantt's leg was cocked grotesquely, and shortened. Santiago began palpating the whole area gently, but with every touch the man groaned. Broken and dislocated femur, which the spasming thigh muscles jammed upward from the acetabulum in the pelvic bone—which itself had been broken. Santiago knew the result, but worked anyway. He might have saved Gantt if the others hadn't hauled him, broken pelvis and all, back to the shack.

"You shouldn't have moved him!" he snapped. And then realized how tired he was. "Sorry. You did what you could. He's dying." The man groaned with even the slightest manipulation. "He's torn up inside," Santiago muttered. "Stomach cavity's filling with blood. Some organs injured."

But before he could consider anything more, traction, splinting, Gantt died. A quick breath, a shudder, silence. Toole worked feverishly pumping the man's lungs, knowing it meant nothing. Every compression of the lungs mauled the internal injuries.

"I didn't help," Toole said wearily, staring at three bearded men. "Don't ever move a man with a broken pelvis. Or a broken neck or back."

They stared at the clay floor. Ignorance had killed Gantt, although he might have died anyway. The woodcutters lowered themselves into tree-stump seats and watched him blankly as he packed his bags.

It was one of those situations he encountered now and then when he couldn't bring himself to ask for a fee. It had cost a day—and had left Miles vulnerable. He let Mick pick his way home and curled into the small, padded buggy seat, trying to sleep. It'd be late, nine or ten, when he got back. At least it had been a real emergency this time, he thought. It seemed an odd comfort, a real emergency. He'd just lost a man. But he dreaded the fraudulent emergency more.

Somehow he slept while his buggy rocked onward behind Mick's steady plodding, and he knew of nothing except the October chill.

A hand shook him, and a voice summoned him.

"Toole!"

Santiago stared up into Pike Garrison's face. Nighttime. Back in Miles. Slowly Santiago swung up in his seat, aware of numbness and icy limbs. He felt he'd lost all the heat in his body.

"I saw your buggy. You sprawled in it."

Toole sat, collecting himself. "I lost a man," he muttered. "Gantt. Woodcutter. Might have saved him if they'd not moved him. Torn up inside. Pelvis broken, and the rest . . . Say, is there trouble here?"

Garrison shook his head. "Quiet enough. Odd night, though."

Toole waited for an explanation.

"If you're not too tired, talk to Kate."

"Mimi all right? The Chinese?"

"Last time I went by."

Santiago turned Mick south on Sixth. The dray switched his tail, protesting, and eyed the doctor dourly as he clambered heavily out of the buggy and into The Stockman. A wall of warmth smacked Santiago. He worked his way through an amiable crowd and found Kate dealing in the rear club room. Looking tired, he thought. They'd threatened her, too. She'd lived with it for weeks. She'd kept her maid Lulu upstairs at the street windows, watching for trouble, but nothing had come. It was the waiting that wore them all down, he thought, as he watched old Boris watch him, and saw the Turk, Ugurplu, glance his direction.

The usual crowd pressed around Kate's table.

"Eddie," she said to her lookout on the laddered stool above. "Take over for a minute. I'll be right back, gents." She smiled at them all, one by one, working her magic, and then steered Santiago toward the rear stairs and privacy.

"Pike said I should talk with you."

She nodded. "I don't think it means anything, but I'd better tell you about it. Tea upstairs? I'm tired."

He followed her up the dark stairwell and into the lamp-lit parlor.

"It's Anna," she began wearily. "The woman came in, through the bar, and set herself down at my table. Pretty early. Still some stools there."

Santiago realized with a start that he'd heard nothing of Anna Waldevsky for several weeks. After Pike had told Peach he intended to enforce the city ordinance, Anna had disappeared from public life.

"Probably half-crazed by that opium syrup."

She nodded. "The woman didn't come to play. All she wanted was to abuse me. She said she could deal as well as I—perfectly true, Dr. Toole. Then she said I'd kept her from dealing—not true, of course. She said I was behind it, that I got you and Pike to keep her from dealing. Blamed me for all her misfortunes. Then she said it was the only thing she wanted to do, deal. She said it was unfair—I can deal but she can't. I tried to explain to her that I have a separate club room, and anyway the law lets me manage my own business. But she didn't see it that way. Doctor, she began raging and crying, and pulling that bottle of stuff out and pouring it down. I . . . I finally had to get Boris to take her . . . but she really raged then, made a scene in front of people.

"I nodded to Boris and he sent someone to Peach, and they came and got her."

"Well, those things happen, Miss Kate."

"That's not all, Doctor. She said she'd get even."

Jubal Peach had a habit of thinking of last straws and rope ends, but in fact he never seemed to come to the end of his rope and his back always supported the additional straw. Even so, his circumstances tortured him, not only at his home but at his club. At home Anna had become a mad dervish. Where once she'd skulked around the darkened place so silent they barely spoke, now she railed at him from the moment he stepped inside to the moment he fled to his clubs.

Always, it came down to one thing: She wanted to deal and couldn't. The law forbade it.

"For once I had some happiness," she wailed. "For once I was having fun—not just sitting around here. For once I wasn't lonely. Men smiled. They liked me and I liked them. I learned how to deal real good. I got to do something. Like the old days, Jubal. Like when I ran away with you."

It started up whenever he stepped in the door. And it swiftly expanded into blame and hate.

"Then they said I couldn't. A woman can't be in a saloon. And it's your law—you had it passed. But that Kate Dubois can. She can stay and deal. They don't make her quit! What's she got that I don't, eh?"

"A private gaming club off the saloon, Anna," he'd told her a dozen times. "And the town's sayin' she can run her business anaway; can't keep her from running a business she owns."

But that had never allayed her complaints. "Not fair!" she howled. "They don't like me! First time I get to do something, they make me stop! You fix it, Jubal. You fix it so I can play. I can't take this sitting around in here no more. You fix it or I'll leave."

He smiled gamely at that. She'd never get a hundred yards from her supply of juice.

"I'm working on it," he'd always told her. "Got to get some tricky business done. Got to get a new sheriff and marshal and justice in without getting myself in trouble.

Maybe I could build a club room for you, back of the Buffalo Hump.''

"I don't want a club room. I want to be out with you, at your layout. You fix this, Jubal, or I'll . . . I'll kill her. She's the one. Flaunting all that good looks and playing the Virgin Mary all the time. Makes me sick. Like no man's ever touched her. She's had twenty. Fifty.''

All this repeated itself daily, indeed several times a day if he happened to wander into his own house several times. It had driven him half-crazy. He gave her all the Williams' Cough Remedy she wanted just to quiet her, but it hardly slowed down that loose tongue.

He'd retreated to the Buffalo Hump and had taken to sleeping there in his office. Anything to avoid her bawling at him. Not that he felt much better in his club. Each night he surveyed the thin crowds and knew Miss Kate had commandeered the trade. He'd patrolled his other saloons and found much the same thing. They filled up on Army paydays and at the end of each month, when the waddies at the surrounding ranches got their cash. But between, trade stayed thin. He told his dealers to increase the edge—they all knew the ways—and told his barmen to use a smaller shot glass and more water. But also to pour an occasional free round, so as not to drive trade out altogether. But it all came to nothing. The Stockman and Miss Kate threatened his entire livelihood.

And still nothing happened. That damned Howitzer kept putting off the main event, the thing that'd bail them all out. One fine, blustery October evening, he summoned Howitzer back to his office and lit a lamp.

"You're delaying. You got those costumes a month ago. You burned the crosses and set up the deal. You got 'em worrying about the Klan. You done it all just right, only nothing happens. I sit here waiting. Trade bleeds away, we all lose. My cannon don't fire. Why don't my cannon shoot, Howitzer?''

The blocky man tipped his bowler back and shrugged, staying silent.

"You ain't talkin'? You want to work for me anamore?"

Howitzer pulled his hat off and clutched it like armor at his breast. "I can't do it," he mumbled.

Peach stared, astounded. "Can't do it? *Can't do it?*"

"She's plumb pretty."

"So are lots of others. Get on with it, Howitzer."

"She's special. Face of a . . . angel."

Peach studied the man, skeptically. Howitzer had buried a few men in the Kansas cattle towns, run hard errands with never a quibble. "This blackmail, Howitzer? You demandin' a little extra this time?"

Howitzer shook his head.

"You ain't even salting her away. Just messing her up a bit. You gone bonkers, Howitzer?"

"Like my sister. Like a girl. She's sweet on me."

"Sweet on you!" Peach guffawed in the gloom. "That's her game, Howitzer. She's sweet on every cowboy and gandy dancer and swaddie from the fort comes in there. She's sweet on the whole world."

"Sweet on me, personal. I seen it in her eye."

"So you don't want to perform a simple task."

Howitzer danced the bowler around through his fingers. "Why don't you do it yourself, Jubal? Since you're so set on it. Maybe you're afraid or anything?"

"I pay you to do it," Peach muttered. "You get your paws dirty for money; I don't."

"You wouldn't want to do it, neither."

Jubal paused, trying to visualize it. In fact he'd enjoy it. He'd enjoy slicing that pretty face into ribbons.

"You gone soft, Howitzer. Maybe I'll put Clem on it. You can have a go at Garrison and Toole and the judge."

"Clem won't do it, neither. He says he's no woman-cutter."

Peach laughed disdainfully. "He's cut up a bunch of dollies."

"Dollies, yes. But he won't cut up a good woman."

Jubal suddenly felt the need. He dug into his desk drawer, uncorked a bottle of Cough Remedy, and swilled, waiting for the peace to steal through him. Confrontation irritated him. He plugged the bottle and returned it, pondering.

"Extra hunnert. I'll pay you now," he said. "You deliver or I'll slit your gullet."

Howitzer shook his head.

Peach wanted to fire the man but something stayed him. Howitzer knew a lot, could talk a lot—if he lived. Peach thought of that empty casket up in the graveyard, and thought how easy it'd be to fill it with Howitzer. A joke on the world.

"Anaway, I can't get my own men to do a job. Mutiny."

"They string a man up for harming a good woman."

That amused Peach. "They string a man up for murder. You done murder a few times, Howitzer."

"I'm not a woman-cutter."

"Looks like I'll have to do it. If I do it, you come along. You and the rest."

Howitzer nodded.

"You get to be Grand Dragon, Howitzer. You wear the boss-sheet. Me, I'll be a ghoul. Wear the ghoul-sheet." It struck Peach funny. Howitzer, the Grand Dragon.

Howitzer nodded. "I'll wear the Grand Dragon one," he said. "But they'll know. They'll figure who's in the sheets."

That puzzled Jubal. "How?"

"Boots. Voice. Back of hands. Rings you wear. Eyes they see. Walk, how we walk."

"It works pretty good in the South. Down there, Klan shows up and everyone's scared blind."

"Just the same, we better get other shoes. And wear gloves. And don't say nothing," Howitzer insisted. "And strange horses, too. Anyone can read a brand. Or figure out who rides what around here."

Jubal smiled. "Maybe they should know. Maybe I want them to know."

"They'll string you up, you hurt her."

Howitzer had a point. Caution . . . Peach sighed. "All right. Tomorrow night. I want you all here at eleven, when the crowd's thinning over there. We'll hit at midnight. Need a few witnessses that get to see the Klan, but not too many.

Don't want to deal with more than a handful. You get some Injun horses out front and ride off after we finish in there. I don't want you running over here. Ride out some and ditch your stuff in the river. Don't all come back at once.''

Howitzer nodded unhappily. ''What about the others? Toole? Garrison?''

''Gets complicated. I'll think about it. Tell you tomorrow night.''

He motioned Howitzer out and settled back in his chair, visualizing the night. He'd never cut anyone before, but a broken beer bottle would make quick work of it. Just take seconds. In and out. Fast, so he could get back to his layout. Like he never left it. Half a block the back way, sixty seconds in The Stockman, and back. Hide the sheet in the vault. Come in through his back door, right into his office. A few seconds, and he'd be King of Miles City again.

Chapter 15

A mean wind whipped out of the north, rattling doors and jabbing icy drafts through window frames. It made an odd rumble in the blued stovepipe rising from the Faultless stove. It drove people off the streets and chilled the play in the Sporting District that night.

Miss Kate had few customers. She considered closing early but a hardy half dozen remained in the club room, five at a poker table and one desultorily bucking her faro game. Another seven drank quietly in the saloon, three at the bar, and four at tables. She'd lose ground tonight. She wouldn't rake in enough to cover wages and expenses.

Wind. It sliced through Miles all year long from every point of the compass. Nothing on the High Plains slowed it down. It lashed buildings in town, making them howl and creak. It drove tumbleweeds down the streets and piled them against fences and buildings. The Stockman became a live thing, resisting wind but groaning and snapping in the gale.

The ticking stove poured out heat, but drafts sucked it away and she felt chilled. She summoned Lulu and asked for her shawl, then dealt another turn. Two, loser, seven, winner. The cowboy's seven won.

"There, Cletus, your luck is good," she said softly, her direct gray eyes on the ruddy boy. She slid two chips out, equaling the ones he'd wagered on the seven. He grinned, meeting her gaze, and pulled the winnings off, letting his bet ride. She adjusted the cases. Three sevens remained, and three more turns.

"It's the wind," he said. "I get lucky when she blows. Drives my bronc crazy, though. He'll pitch all the way out."

Cletus bunked eight miles west and faced a long ride out to the ranch.

"You could stay in Miles tonight. I'd feel better if you did."

Lulu brought her knitted shawl and Kate settled it over her shoulders, feeling warmer at once. The yellow went nicely with her white blouse, black velvet choker, and the canary ribbon in her hair. Her dealers wore heavy waistcoats tonight to ward off the chill. She didn't permit them to wear suit coats.

Cold weather would slow things down. Miles roared through the summer and quieted through the bitter Montana winters, except when the chinooks blew. A good warm chinook combined with a fort payday, or month-end pay at the ranches, could momentarily blazon the Sporting District even in the depths of winter. But even so, trade nearly died during the cold months.

She'd made it. She could weather it now. She'd paid off Pericles Shaw and still had garnered seventeen hundred, and most evenings added a bit more to her bank. Not enough to run all her games. Not enough to run high-stakes games. She kept her maximum bets clamped low, especially on the roulette wheel where a lucky streak and high-odds bets could ruin her. She wouldn't add much to her bank through the winter, but next spring . . .

She played the last turn and showed the hock, a seven, and shuffled, settling them in the case box again and turning over the soda.

But her cowboy was done. "Guess I'll buck the breeze, Miss Kate," he said, pushing his chips to her. He'd won seven dollars, which she paid from a cash drawer.

"Come again, Cletus. It was fun to have you here."

"You're my gal, Miss Kate."

He grinned wistfully at her, buttoned his sheepskin coat, and braved the howling night.

She snapped open the cover of her watch, which hung

from a ribboned clip at her waist, and discovered the hands at eleven-thirty. Not late. Some nights the play had just begun at this hour. She eyed the ones at the poker table. A cowboy, two corporals, and a sergeant. She rented tables for a small fee and made money on drinks. At other tables she had a house dealer, sometimes herself.

She gazed at her establishment amiably. Boris dozed on a stool at the club room door, keeping an eye on things through catnaps. Itzak Ugurplu slouched on a barstool, looking bored. She thought about letting him go early but decided not to. Those Klan threats, not to mention Jubal Peach's bitterness, had hung over her through the fall, and she'd promised herself never to let down her guard. At first these things had wearied her. She'd lost sleep. But nothing came of them. It had been a perverse joke.

Restlessly she abandoned her table and wandered through The Stockman, down the long, glowing rosewood bar to the front window. Outside, in the dim window light, she discovered eight or nine rawboned horses at the hitch rail. More horses than out-of-town customers, she thought, smiling primly. Those shy cowboys often tied their broncs to her hitch rail and then visited the parlor houses down the street. The knowledge amused her.

Off toward the center of town the fire bell clanged, its strident clamor mixing with the moan of the wind so that she wasn't sure it rang at all. In the saloon men lifted their heads uncertainly. The wind played tricks. And yet the clamor persisted. A fire somewhere, and a windy night, too. Danger. Miles city had been built with pine planks and two-by-fours cut up the Tongue River.

She stepped outside into the gale and peered anxiously north toward Main Street, into the wind, the direction of danger. Nothing. Blackness. But off east she thought she discerned a yellow glow. Hard to tell. She stepped back inside, shivering.

"Itzak," she said, "you'd better go find out."

The Turk nodded and shrugged into his greatcoat.

Around her men drank up, laid coin and bills on the bar,

and tugged on their coats. A fire bell commanded them. On a windy night the whole town could burn to the ground. In the club room the poker players abandoned their hand, retrieved their chips from the pot, hastily evened things up, and plunged into the howling night. In moments only a cripple, old Josh, and three stove-up old pensioners in from the ranches remained.

She heard shouting outside, and the passage of horses and men. From the front window she saw a distinct glow in the southeast, over near the warehouse along the NP tracks. The Chinese Quarter, she thought, her throat constricting.

Itzak burst in with news. "China Quarter on fire. On purpose. Someone splashed coal oil and lit it. And they say a flaming cross, Miss Kate."

Fear lanced her. She peered around her empty club. Old Boris had unfolded from his stool and stood alert. Her barman, Portneuf, stood expectantly in front of the mirrored backbar.

"We'll close. I want this place dark and locked in five minutes. Itzak, grab a pail and go fight it. And keep your eye peeled. You're my eyes and ears outside."

Itzak pulled a tin bucket from under the bar and plunged into the howling night. Her two dealers followed.

Now she'd close. And when the club was dark and locked she and Boris would sit quietly in the gloom, armed, watching front and rear doors.

The old ranch men heard her and tugged out coins from their pockets to settle their tabs. Off somewhere in the windy night the fire bell clanged imperiously.

She peered out the window and saw nothing. And then something. White apparitions running toward her, ghosts, ghouls, creatures with conical headpieces and flowing robes, angels of doom. Coming.

She screamed, and snapped the bolt on the front door. But the rear boomed open, shooting a blast of cold into The Stockman. One stood there in the wavering light of wind-whipped lamps, one white death-angel staring at her from holes in his high mask, unknown eyes from the pits of hell.

She screamed. The others reached the locked front door and battered it. Glass shattered. The door burst inward, slamming on its hinges. The old ranchers gasped. Five white dervishes poured in, their peaked headgear making them all seven feet tall. All carried weapons in gloved hands, four black revolvers and a shotgun.

Boris whipped his hand into his coat.

"Don't," said one masked man, pointing the shotgun straight at the old Russian.

Boris slowly eased his hand out, looking trapped.

Portneuf carefully raised his hands, helpless under the bores of so many revolvers.

Kate whirled toward the rear, toward her apartment. Upstairs. Lulu slept up there. Get up there. Lock that door and shoot if they tried . . .

She ran. She had to duck that one, that looming one at the rear, the one standing there with two broken green bottles in his black-gloved hands.

She stared at him. At the broken bottles. He filled the doorway. Behind her the white-robed ghosts, weightless phantasms, poured into the club room. One had a red-and-black insignia, an embroidered circlet of some kind, on the breast of the robe he wore. Three floated in, stalking around her, ghost wolves, apparitions whose footsteps she couldn't hear, as if they floated an inch from the floor.

She spun dizzily as the circle tightened, these white ghosts closing from four sides, closing down upon her.

Then two grabbed her. She grappled with them, squirming and dodging, but she was no match for the iron grips that pinioned her. She writhed, but she writhed against jail bars. She bit and yelled and tugged. Outside of the club room Boris roared and started toward her. A shot. Silence. Acrid powder smoke drifting past a chandelier.

Three held her now. She could see unblinking eyes in those holes. Eyes she knew yet didn't know. They pulled her, dragged her toward her faro table, hoisted her onto it, knocking the tiger case box to the ground. Her world whirled. She smelled cigars. The one who'd burst through the rear door sprang toward her, lifted the broken whiskey bottles, and then she knew. She knew an instant before her body knew.

And all she knew was Scream. . . .

The fire bell reached into Santiago's stupor, demanding and coaxing. He awakened, listening, drugged with young sleep. He turned to drift off again, but the clamor wouldn't let him. He yawned, willing himself awake. Alertness didn't come. He swung his legs to the floor, waiting for energy. Mimi stirred, reached for him, and rolled over. They'd been in bed scarcely an hour. But trouble came whenever it came and plucked doctors and sheriffs out of warm beds.

He heard his cottage groan in the wind, heard windows chatter in frames, felt air eddying through the bedroom. Wind. Fire. The recognition jolted energy into him. Nothing fell more deadly upon a town built of matchsticks than fire and wind. He dragged black britches over his nightshirt, realized he'd need his longhandles in that cold, and started over. Three minutes later and still feeling rattle-headed, he pulled his revolver belt around him and picked up his Gladstone bag. He didn't know what he'd be this night—doctor or sheriff. He found his wool greatcoat and shrugged into it, feeling clumsy, and pushed out the door into a cold gale.

Blackness. He groped his way toward Main Street, seeing nothing. But the bell clamored. There on Main, shadowy men hurried east. He followed them, discerning at last a glow in the southeastern quarter of town. Chang Loon! He sprinted that way, cutting south on Ninth, seeing flames ahead and an eerie mob passing buckets through amber light. Chang's store blazed, and before it a wooden cross blazed, too. Fierce wind whipped the flames southward, igniting a string of small low houses like Chinese firecrackers.

Breathlessly he pushed through the milling fire brigade, looking for Garrison, for explanations, for Chang Loon, one of the two or three Celestials who could speak enough English to tell him what had happened. As if he needed an explanation, he thought bitterly. Burned out, and with winter coming on.

He found Chang standing upwind of the fire, as immobile as a carved statue except for his pigtail, which lashed like a tiger's tail in the bitter wind.

"Chang! Are any hurt?"

The Chinese shook his head. Slowly he pointed at a huddle of people, mostly in black. "All there," he said.

"Who did it, Chang? You see anyone?"

Fear caught the man and he gazed silently toward the wavering earth. "No," he said at last. "They gone when we see fire."

"Chang! My God . . ."

The little store's roof was collapsing with a roar, sending spark-showers whirling into the inky vortex. The little carmine-walled store had been the center of Chinese life in Miles, the place to buy Chinese greens and incense and rice and high-collared cotton jackets and wooden clogs.

"Chang—take them to the jail. That's all I've got. That and the courthouse."

The tall slender man nodded somberly.

Toole watched the crowd at work, marveling as always at the organized way a crowd puts out a fire. Lines had formed from the two hand-pumps in the area, where men jacked the handles furiously and splashed water into buckets that were handed along to those at the fire. Half of them, he knew, hated Celestials, and probably thought they were doing it to save the warehouse beyond. But it didn't matter—they fought the fires ferociously.

He spotted Garrison, his Greener tucked under his arm, patrolling the whole chaotic scene, glaring fiercely at half-dressed men, some of whom might have deliberately started this roaring inferno.

"Pike!"

The marshal bulled through the fire lines to Santiago. "They did it. Waited until we thought it'd died out," Pike growled.

"We'll get them, Pike. Even if we have to haul every South-bred man in town into the jail for some hard questions."

Pike grinned sourly. "You'll need more than that, Doc."

Doc Santiago sighed. When they called the sheriff of Custer County "Doc", they were saying something about him. It'd never go away. No matter what he accomplished as sheriff, he'd be "Doc" to most of them. Not a real sheriff.

Someone in a greatcoat shouted at him from across a bucket line. The Turk. Miss Kate's saloon man. Santiago threaded his way through sweating men, smelling char in the eddying whorls of air and feeling the blister of flame on his face.

The Turk looked wild-eyed. "Doctor. Come! It's Miss Kate! They came!"

Toole could barely understand it. The thing hit him at the base of his stomach. Ugurplu tugged at him, grabbed his arm.

"Pike!" he cried. "The Stockman! Kate! I've got to go! Take care of these people! The jail, the courthouse . . ."

"Hurry, Dr. Toole."

Garrison gaped, and then nodded. Santiago wheeled westward behind the trotting saloon man, hoping he had all he needed in his Gladstone bag, fearing the worst. Thank God he had Garrison now, he thought. A few weeks earlier he'd have faced the two disasters alone.

His lungs labored in the icy wind and cold damp air caught in his bellows, winding him. And still he trotted behind the Turk down Bridge Street until The Stockman loomed black out of the night. To the south parlor house lanterns swayed and wavered on their bails, emitting hellish glows.

The shattered door of the club gaped open, a black cave beyond. But not black. Lamps glowed in the club room. He heard a strange, piercing screaming, as monotonous as a train whistle shrilling unstopped. Icy air eddied through the club. He fumbled his way through the darkened saloon . . . and found Voroshlikov sprawled on the floor, his mouth grinning, his eyes staring sightlessly. He jerked to a halt, knelt, found no pulse. He pressed his ear to the man's chest and heard nothing. Toole felt wetness on his ear. Blood.

He sprang up and staggered into the club room where the

keening rose, unabated. On the faro table . . . there . . . Kate, lying. He crept close, dread and revulsion gripping him, seeing and not wanting to see the red pulp that had been her face. Off in a corner Lulu sobbed. The barman, Portneuf, stared helplessly.

Paralysis took him. He couldn't organize himself, couldn't even decide what to do. He stared. Her wail ground out of her gaping, butchered lips unceasingly, renewed with each ragged breath. Red sheeted over her whole face and dripped onto the green faro layout. Great gouges welled bright blood. One down the center of her forehead. Another angling across an eyebrow, slicing through an eyelid, down across the side of her nose, baring cartilege, cutting the nostril, slashing through both lips and down past the chin. A piece of scalp hung loose, blood oozing from under it. An ear lobe dangling. One vicious gouge down her neck, over the carotid— he studied it, not seeing the pump of blood there—across her throat. And more. A hundred slashes more.

He didn't know where to begin. The terrible wail rattled his sleep-rattled head. The vital signs. He dug for his stethoscope and pressed it, trembling, on her chest. The slightest touch drove her wailing to crescendo. Heart rapid but strong. Breathing short, with an obscure gurgle. Alive and likely to remain so, unless infection took her.

Not fatal cuts. But that eye. The gouge cut straight down across the eyeball. So much blood he could scarcely see the butchery underneath. Cold air numbing his fingers.

"Madam," he snapped at the maid. "Shut the rear door. Build up that fire." He turned toward the barman. "Close that front door. Then stand guard. You have a weapon under the bar."

The man sprang to action.

"I want hot water. Clean cloth. Kitchen pots. And then fetch Mrs. Toole. I'll need her for the chloroform."

The tear-stained woman nodded.

Santiago rolled up his sleeves, a hard dark calm sliding into him. Medicine first. And then the law, with all its fury. Men would hang before he'd finished.

He found cold water and soap in the dry sink at the saloon and washed with it, eyeing bottles of antiseptic lined along the backbar. He found a pan and poured carbolic in it, added water, and rinsed his hands in it carefully. How well she healed depended on his care now.

He carried the carbolic solution back to the wailing woman and studied her, dreading that diagonal gash more than the rest. The room warmed slightly and the numbness fled his hands. He touched her head, turning it, looking for lacerations in back of her ear. She screeched, a howl that rose from that primeval place where all the sorrows of woman are borne. He soaked a ball of cotton in carbolic and dabbed blood away from her nose, where it gouted into her nasal cavity and threatened her breathing. She sobbed. He switched to cotton soaked in whiskey.

Her hands flew upward to ward him off, knocking the cotton from his fingers. Blood puddled in her left eye socket, leaked steadily down her slashed cheeks, and pooled on the painted deuce.

"Kate! Kate! It's Dr. Toole."

She howled, half a sob and half a desolated groan.

"Kate! You'll be all right! These cuts . . . these, they're only skin-deep. All but one. Skin-deep."

"Skin-deep," she muttered, and sobbed in gurgling gasps such as he'd never heard in all his practice.

Chapter 16

It seemed forever before Mimi arrived. He'd done what he could beforehand, boiling instruments, needles, and cloths on the parlor stove, asking for full lamps—many a surgery had been imperiled by a failing lamp—and preparing a mild solution of permanganate of potash, a gentle antiseptic.

He could not touch Kate without triggering paroxysms of screaming and flailing arms. Her bleeding had slowed and seemed not to pose a danger. He'd soothed her while he prepared, talked quietly about the future, about healing, about whatever came to his head, but he couldn't tell whether she heard or cared or understood. He pitied her, but didn't have time to dwell on it. These lacerations scored her soul more deeply than her face. The sheriff part of him kept intruding, running down lists of suspects, of which Jubal Peach stood at the top. He had to put her under and then sew her together delicately, with tiny stitches and thin, sterilized silk thread to leave as few scars on her lovely face as possible. For that, he wanted her inert.

He couldn't use ether, not with lamps blazing around the faro table. He could dope her with morphia or he could render her senseless with chloroform. He always dreaded the chloroform, an irritating anesthetic easily over-administered and potentially fatal, causing heart stoppage. It degenerated into a lethal gas, phosgene, that smelled like musty hay when it came into contact with the lamps or sunlight, and on occasion, during a long surgery, Santiago had suffered grave headaches, sore throats, and dizziness from the toxic gas. He trusted only one person, Mimi, to administer it, holding a saturated pad of it to the nose of the patient while keeping a sharp eye on pulse and breath.

Mimi burst through the front door to find herself staring into the bore of Portneuf's shotgun for a long tense moment, then slid back to the club room, her dark eyes absorbing everything in moments and her gaze resting on the mutilated, bloodstained face of Kate Dubois. Kate's maid Lulu followed, still weeping through the terrible evening.

"Who, Santo?"

"Men in sheets."

"I—Mon Dieu! Oh, oh, Kate."

"Start taking her down, Mimi," he said softly.

She nodded and slipped her heavy coat off, studying the woman on the faro table. Mimi's jet hair hung loose and she'd thrown on a brown dress. Santiago began his scrubbing, soap and water first and then mild carbolic solution. Not that it mattered much, he thought, staring at facial lacerations cut by dirty, shattered bottles.

The eerie howling still went on and on. Kate threw her head back and forth until Santiago gripped it while Mimi administered the pungent, volatile liquid. But whenever Mimi brought the chloroform pad close to the raw flesh of Kate's nose and butchered lips she went berserk. That half-severed nostril hurt most of all, and was so sensitive that Kate bucked and heaved when Mimi pressed the pad close. Nowhere did the human body have a denser collection of nerves than around the nostrils, as Santiago well knew. Mimi might not be able to anesthetize her.

For a half hour, to the toll of Kate's sobbing, they tried the chloroform, but Kate's swollen, sliced nose kept them from succeeding.

Time was flying by and he still hadn't gotten to the dirty wounds, hadn't cleaned and sutured them.

Mimi peered up and shook her head.

Morphia then. He prepared a minimal injection, not happy, knowing it wouldn't put Kate out.

"This will make the pain go away, Kate," he said, jabbing

the sterilized needle into her triceps. The small dose, equal to a sixth of a grain, would take ten or fifteen minutes to calm her. An overdose of morphia could cause respiratory failure, so he preferred to go small and slow. Kate's soft sobbing never ceased. Mimi took the chloroform-saturated pads to the rear door and tossed them outside, letting in a blast of arctic air.

One advantage to the gale, he thought: It would sweep the gas out. But the eddying fresh air left his hands so numb he wondered how he'd suture the wounds.

Kate stopped her moaning and something peaceful settled over her brown-crusted face. He slid onto the faro table and lifted Kate by the shoulders until her head lay in his lap.

He touched her head, tentatively, and she let him. He began dabbing the crusted blood and grit away with a whiskey-soaked ball of cotton, but when he approached that long diagonal gash, she groaned.

Kate remained conscious, aware, but passive at last, and he began to deal with the terrible lacerations one by one. Mimi held Kate's head up while he irrigated the gouged eye socket. He got it clean enough to see the wound itself, which cut through the eyebrow, half severed the eyelid, scraped across the eyeball—but not through the sclerotic membrane and into the darker choroid, and missing the cornea. He found shards of bottle glass and tweezered them out. The area had already swollen. From there the gash cut down the side of her nose, baring gristle, and cut clear through a nostril—the *crus laterale cartilaginis apicis*, he thought crazily—and downward, severing the upper lip and slicing into the lower one.

"Will she lose her eye, Santo?"

"I don't know. I don't think so. Didn't reach the vitreous humor."

"Thank God," Mimi muttered. "The poor thing."

He touched Kate's nose where the nostril had been cut and she screamed. He wished he could anesthetize her, but he lacked the means. Not even a heavy dose of morphia would numb the pain there. No wonder Mimi couldn't get much chloroform into her.

Through the night he labored, while Mimi helped, holding the woman, clamping Kate's head while Santiago sutured wound after wound as delicately as he could with a fine needle and slender silk. A furrow down her brow that exposed bone he sewed tight. A flap of scalp he tacked down. But he couldn't touch her severed nostril or her upper lip without evoking an eerie wail, rising deep from Kate's stupor. Wearily he soaked his sutures with permanganate of potash, staining Kate's flesh purple. He sewed gently, each stitch a prayer for her beauty, pulling lacerated flesh together in whatever way would leave the tiniest scar. But her slashed upper lip and half-severed nostril stymied him. These he dabbed with antiseptic as best he could while Kate writhed and screamed, and then covered the other wounds with gauze pads and plasters, hoping for the best. She would look harelipped, and her nose might be grotesque. Once he injected more morphia, worrying about the dose.

His hands felt numb again. "Build up that fire!" he snapped, weariness engulfing him. And still some suturing remained. He began to tack a torn lobe back upon her left ear, and to clean the long, deep gash that had barely missed her carotid. Sometime in the night he noticed the broken green bottles lying on the floor, next to the canary ribbon that had tied her hair. Evidence, he thought. Green bottles exactly like thousands of other green bottles. He didn't care about the sheriffing; he cared only for Kate's health and beauty, and his fingers worked prayers and voiced petitions to Kate's flesh while Santiago's soul voiced petitions to God.

"Santo. You love her."

She said it without guile, but he sensed her insecurity.

He smiled wearily. "Everyone loves Kate. I want to give her whatever I have."

From within his grip on her head Kate slurred out words. "Iss over," she said. "Over."

"Not over, Miss Kate. You're a strong, beautiful woman."

She wept from the one eye that could leak tears.

At three Garrison appeared, interrupting him, studying Kate's ghastly, purple-stained face and noting Boris Voroshlikov, still sprawled on the floor of the saloon. Wordlessly the marshal set to work, carrying Boris into the night and over to Tobias's.

Santiago scarcely noticed, but when Garrison returned he found himself full of questions.

"Where's Chang Loon, Pike?"

"The parlor house women took them all in, Toole. Every one."

The outcasts caring for the outcasts, Santiago thought, but didn't say it.

"Fire's dead?"

"Few coals. I've got a couple of volunteers watching. But with the north wind . . ."

"Question them?"

"Yeah. They didn't see nothing. Chang had to translate. They found the fire, the burning cross. No one around."

"Diversion. Burn out the Chinese for a diversion," Santiago muttered.

"You figure the target was here, eh?"

Santiago still sat on the faro table, cradling Kate's head in his lap while he sutured and cleaned. "I figure they wanted Kate, and I figure it has nothing to do with the Klan. But I can't prove it. Tomorrow I'm going to haul Peach in and shake him until his bones rattle. I'm going to shut him down. I'm going to—"

"Peesh," Kate slurred through her swollen lips.

"Kate? You know that?"

"Cigar breath."

"Did they say anything, Kate?"

She shook her head faintly, too groggy to respond.

He turned first to Portneuf and then Lulu, who watched wearily. "Who do you think it was?"

The barman shook his head. "Happened too fast. White sheets. All I saw was a lot of sheets and pointy white hats. Boris . . . They shot him when he tried to help. . . . I was so scared—thought I'd be next. Closed my eyes waiting for a bullet.''

"Boris?'' mumbled Kate.

Santiago paused, staring into the wavering flames of the lamps, not wanting to answer.

"We'll talk about Boris later.''

"Dead. I'm dead, too.''

Santiago thought it might be true.

Santiago sulked in his office through the rest of the night, too tired and angry to sleep, his mind chewing on questions. He'd carried Kate up to her apartment and settled her in her bed, with Lulu's help. He'd wrapped her head, including her eyes, leaving only her slashed nose and mouth uncovered. He had to cover her good eye, because eyes worked together and he wanted as little eyeball motion as possible. Kate lay blind.

He had stood in the lamplight feeling a terrible pity for her, and fear as well, for there'd be only Lulu to guard Kate. The barman had left. Kate lay in a stupor, much too heavily sedated with morphia, but he couldn't help it. He'd left her to the weary maid and lurched home with Mimi, through an icy blackness that hinted of a harsh winter. She'd plunged back into their warm bed, but he'd settled himself in the rocker and waited for dawn to loom out of the east, shotgun across his lap, defying those ghouls to strike at his dear Mimi, or himself.

His first impulse was to commandeer Garrison, then drag Jubal Peach out of his bed and haul him down to the jail and let him stew there. Santiago's red-eyed rage prodded him that direction, but in the end he resisted. It would accomplish nothing and would be improper. Not that he cared about propriety. No. He hadn't a shred of evidence other than cigar breath. Plus an obvious motive. But motives didn't convict. He would question the saloon men at the Buffalo Hump and would come up with nothing. They would all report that Peach had been around all night, either at his faro layout or in his office.

Still, Santiago would get to the bottom of this thing. He'd turn the whole town upside down doing it. He'd skin his fists doing it. He'd break rules doing it. But he would do it, even if it meant pounding the truth out of Peach and his uglies. By blue dawn he'd become a cauldron of seething rage, boiling to strike. By early light he'd decided he'd grab Howitzer for starters and ransack the Buffalo Hump. At seven, while Mimi yet slept, he stalked out into the silver morning, his face stubbled and his eyes bagged, and hammered on the door of Pericles Shaw. By seven-thirty he had a hand-written warrant in hand and stalked toward the Buffalo Hump in cold air and flat light, ready for murder.

Howitzer's small lean-to apartment lay to the rear of the Buffalo Hump and he started there, rapping on the white-washed plank door with the barrel of his Peacemaker, splintering pine. So much Irish rage boiled through him he scarcely noticed his exhaustion. Howitzer, sleepy and in a gray nightshirt, opened.

"I'm taking you in for questioning," Santiago snapped.

Howitzer examined the huge bore of the weapon aimed at his middle, and acceded.

"Both hands in front of you."

He manacled one wrist, keeping the bore of his revolver under Howitzer's nose, and then the other, defying the thick thug to try anything, anything at all.

"What's this all about, Toole?"

Toole kicked Howitzer in the bare shin.

"Not nice, Toole."

Santiago ignored him and barged in, found Howitzer's britches, and found a key to the Buffalo Hump in them. He shoved Howitzer onto his skinny bed and ransacked the place, looking for sheets, for gloves, for blood. He pulled drawers and dumped contents on the plank floor, kicking shirts and linens and cravats and black stockings. He found Howitzer's small revolver and sniffed. It had been fired, but he couldn't tell how long ago. Not cleaned. He pulled the cylinder, looking for spent shells, and found none. He yanked dirty linens from a pile of used clothing and smelled horse and crap. He yanked Howitzer off the bed and onto the floor, threw off a blanket and a grimy sheet, and then lifted the whole straw-filled tick, spraying bedbugs. Howitzer watched sourly.

"Where's the sheets, Howitzer?"

Howitzer smiled, getting cocky.

Toole kicked him hard.

"Get up. We're going into the club."

Howitzer didn't move. Toole pulled his boot back, and Howitzer scrambled up. They walked outside, Howitzer's legs chalky below his nightshirt, and into the Buffalo Hump's rear door. The place lay heavy in sepia morning shadow and stank of beer and cigars.

"Where were you last night? Account for every minute," Toole said, shoving Howitzer into Peach's gloomy office.

"Here."

"Open that!" Toole roared, pointing at Peach's gray safe.

"I can't."

Toole punched him.

"I can't!"

Toole kicked him.

"I'll kill you, Toole."

"I'll take note of it."

Toole yanked open desk drawers and threw the contents of closets onto the geometric avocado-and-copper patterns of the carpet. Nothing.

"Who killed Boris?"

"Don't know what you're talking about."

Toole smacked him.

"Who killed Boris?"

"I don't know."

Toole kicked him, a vicious blow to the shin.

"Ow!"

"Who cut her?"

"I don't know."

Toole's fist caught Howitzer, knocking him to the filthy floor. Howitzer groaned, rolled in the dirt, and stayed down, eyes wary.

"Who cut her?"

Howitzer pulled himself into a ball.

Toole booted him. "Who cut her?"

Howitzer grunted and pulled his arms over his head, saying nothing.

"Where'd the Klan sheets come from?"

"Klan? What Klan?"

The answer sounded too smart. Toole booted him.

"You torch the Chinese?"

Howitzer cringed.

"You plant that cross on my lawn, Howitzer? Got something against Irish? Or breeds?"

Howitzer rolled into a tighter sphere.

"Get up."

Howitzer refused.

"Walk to your room. Maybe I'll free you. I've got other business."

Howitzer peered up, rolled to his feet, and walked. Toole unlocked the manacles and shoved him onto his bed. He kept Howitzer's revolver and confiscated a knout and knife as well.

"I'll be back for you, Howitzer."

"I'll be waiting, Toole," the man said, rubbing shins.

Toole slammed the door behind him and kept the key to the saloon for future use.

He rounded a corner and ran into Peach, whose derringer poked into Toole's chest.

Peach smiled. "I thought you was a burglar, Toole," he said. "Place is torn up in there."

"I tore it."

"You got some reason?"

"Search warrant. Where's your sheet, Peach?"

"Sheet? Sheet? Balance sheet?"

"Put that popgun down. You're threatening the law."

Peach smiled amiably and slid it back into the breast of his frock coat. "You have something against me, Sheriff?"

"Where were you last night? Every damned minute."

"Right here, Toole."

"I'll check it. Who were your customers?"

"How should I know? Almost none. Quiet night. A few sergeants."

"Describe them."

"Three chevrons, Toole."

Santiago stopped himself from pounding the man.

"Who's your alibi?"

"Alibi? Has there been a crime?"

"Too smart, Peach. That's too smart."

"I seek only knowledge, Toole. May I light a cigar?"

"No."

"Has there been a crime?"

Tiredness engulfed Santiago. Whatever had sustained his weary body drained out of him, leaving an exhausted hulk.

"All right, Peach. All right. I'm going to prove it. I'll string you up before this is done. You and Howitzer back there, and the rest."

"String us up?"

"By the neck until dead, Peach. You're living on borrowed time."

"Anaway, I'd better see a lawyer," Peach said. "The law seems to be prejudiced."

"It is," Toole said.

Chapter 17

An expectant darkness settled upon Miles City, as if the prairie town lived under an eclipsed sun. No one supposed it was all over, least of all Santiago.

He took it upon himself to bury Boris Voroshlikov in the graveyard up on the bluff. It turned out that the old man had a considerable estate, over three thousand dollars in The Stockmen's and Drover's Bank. He had Pericles Shaw appoint him executor and used a little of the money to employ Sylvane Tobias's services. So once again Tobias's awesome black hearse wound its majestic way through town, this time with a real burden. Men grieved. Boris had been a respected, if mysterious, part of the community. Santiago knew of no Orthodox cleric anywhere in the Territory, so he conducted a simple ceremony, a prayer for the departed. A eulogy. Something to memorialize the dead man and commend him to God. Many came, listened silently, and departed. Back in his office afterward, Santiago set out at once to locate relatives by publishing notices in a variety of places in New York as well as the Territory. He doubted that anyone would claim the money. As a last resort he wrote the Russian embassy, on the slim chance that its diplomatic staff might be able to discover Voroshlikov's relatives across the endless sea.

The burned-out Chinese fared a little better, thanks to the help of the parlor house women, who instinctively opened their purses to other outcasts. Even while the earth beneath the burnt buildings remained warm, Chang Loon and his fellow Celestials patiently cleared away ash and rubble and

164

began to rebuild. Santiago made a point of helping; stood at hand quietly, and dealt fiercely with various townsmen, especially merchants, who wanted to drive the Celestials out, use their land, clear Miles of the taint of heathen.

The worst of these was Tobias, who scolded Toole at every opportunity.

"Those Chinamen don't belong here. Dirty devils, grubbing a living, keeping respectable men from getting decent jobs. Heathen. This here's white man territory."

"Sylvane, one more word out of you I'll pound you, so help me God. They've a right to be here and a right to survive. They got burned out and you haven't an ounce of sympathy in your mean heart. Those people raise most of the fresh vegetables here, milk and eggs, do laundry, sell firewood—I buy cords of it from them. Work hard, live quietly. And now you want to add more misery."

"Heathen," retorted Tobias. "I can hardly stand even to plant them up on the hill. Off in a far corner of the graveyard."

Santiago had stormed out, not wanting to hear more.

Twice a day, mornings and afternoons, Santiago gathered his courage together and walked to the quiet, dark Stockman and let himself in the rear door. Downstairs, in the saloon and club room, dust settled over bottles and tables. The blood on Kate's faro layout turned brown and crusty. Another brown bloodstain soaked the varnished planks where Boris had fallen. Deep shadows hung in the place and stayed there, claiming victory. A vague smell of must and fetid air filled the silent rooms.

Kate had only Lulu, who hovered soundlessly upstairs, her face gray and drawn. The first two days he kept Kate sedated with laudanum, as much as he hated to do it. She lay quietly, saying nothing, unable to see because of the heavy bandaging over both eyes. Her lips and nose had become infected and swollen, and looked awful. Lulu could scarcely get broth into her through lips so torn. Santiago could do little except hold Kate's hand for a while, sometimes talking of a good life to come but mostly knowing it sounded like lies to her. She said nothing, her soul and mind vanished to some place far away.

The third day he discovered fever and also smelled putrescence beneath those bandages. He could do little. Old-time doctors called it benevolent pus, but he knew it was only the detritus of infection and there was nothing benevolent about it. Her face was infected, and the infections would leave their own scars on top of the lacerations. The infection could even kill her if it got out of hand. He debated removing the dressings and cleaning the wounds, but decided against it. Many a doctor had ruined healing by interfering with the human body's own repairs. All he'd be able to do was to dab antiseptics on the surfaces of wounds, anyway. He had nothing to allay the flaming infection raging deep in her flesh.

So that, too, became a vigil. He waited. The town waited and wondered. A few brave citizens ventured to ask him about Kate's progress and prognosis, and Santiago could only shake his head. Rumors drifted to him. Out on the ranches, it was said, cowboys had turned hard and were talking of nooses and lynchings. Soldiers in blue bunches walked silently past the darkened Stockman night after night, staring into its somber gloom and muttering. One day two sergeants came to him with five hundred dollars.

"We raised this over at the post. It's a reward, Sheriff. All the fellows kicked in, and glad to do it, too. You make a sign that says there's five hundred dollars reward for . . . You know how to word it. Information, all that. Whoever cut up Kate."

Santiago accepted it, strangely touched, and had posters printed. Everywhere he nailed them up people gathered and stared.

At home Mimi belabored him about his safety.

"You're next, Santo. I know it."

"Could be," he agreed. He stayed armed now, even on his medical calls, when he traditionally carried no weapons. But the revolver in its black leather pouch at his side offered no comfort at all. If anyone meant to kill him the task would get done. A shot from any rooftop or window or false front, as he did his rounds, would finish him. He glared relentlessly at upper windows and roofs as he walked these days, always finding nothing. And yet the town seemed to hang on the brink of cataclysm.

Mimi herself carried a derringer wherever she went, knowing what the Klan did to anyone not all white. She'd turned dour, and slammed through her chores with glittering eyes and an angry spirit. Whenever she had a free moment she stalked south, crossed Main, and delivered wicker baskets full of her fresh bread to the Celestials, who toiled at reconstruction from pre-dawn to post-dark, desperately in need of homes and shops before bitter winter closed down on them.

If Santiago worried about a sniper's bullet aimed at himself, he worried even more about one aimed at Pike Garrison, who patrolled the West End in the dark of the night, where any assassin could hover unseen on a roof or behind a false front.

"Pike," he said, "let's do the rounds together at night. We need the two of us."

"Doc, you're tired. Getting up before dawn to do your own rounds. In fact I've been worrying about you, out there alone."

"Things quiet, Pike?"

The town marshal pondered it. "In a way. But not really. In the Buffalo Hump they know they've won. Howitzer's cocky. That big galoot Walden sits at the bar and grins. Peach's smily. And he's got Anna dealing again."

"Anna?"

"Yeah, dealing. She's gussied up. Henna hair, lots of Anna showing. She sips stuff from a whiskey glass, but it's not whiskey and she looks bad. She sure's happy, though. Smiles a lot."

"Peach's flaunting her. Daring you to do something."

Pike's face darkened. "If I nip him, or her, I'm dead. That's what they want; what they're waiting for. Always three or four, Howitzer and the rest, smirking."

The challenge. Santiago stared out upon leaden clouds,

wondering how it'd end up. "Pike. Stay away from there for now."

"Hate to be taken for a coward, Doc."

"Be brave and dead, then."

Garrison nodded. "You got any ideas?"

"Not any good ones. I'm hoping Kate will reopen in a couple of weeks."

"They'd just go at her again."

"Yes," said Santiago. "Yes. That's what I'm thinking."

That afternoon he decided to change Kate's dressings. Her fever had broken, and the wounds open to air had scabbed over. He stuffed his Gladstone with fresh sterile bandaging and walked over there in a nippy afternoon wind. He found her sitting up, her eyes still blinded by the dressings.

"Kate. It's time to have a look."

She didn't respond.

He settled gently on the edge of her bed and began snipping white cotton away. The rank smell of pus rose out of the old dressings, and after cutting away a layer he found the yellow and gray stains of suppuration in the cloth. The smell gagged him.

He remembered that he should protect her eyes, and walked to the window to draw its curtains. Still too much light, so he pulled a sepia coverlet from the bed and hung it over the curtain rod. The bedroom slipped into a gloom safe for recently unbandaged eyes.

Her slim hands clenched and unclenched the blankets as he cut, but she said nothing at all. He pulled away the upper wraps and her hair tumbled free, greasy with a week's oils. He unwound cloth from her forehead and found it had stuck to her wounds. He snipped around the plastered fabric and continued to unwind, until at last a yellow heap of foul bandage lay on the floor and Kate blinked at him from eyes that had seen nothing for eight days. What he saw as he looked into them was not life or joy, but hell.

The injured eye was encased in swollen flesh and looked grotesque, a squeezed purple lemon in her eye socket. But she was seeing him with it, although no doubt with blurred or grotesque vision. Her other gray eye focused on him. The injured eye socket still suppurated and looked angry, with red streaks radiating outward to her cheek and nose. Her slashed eyelid had begun to knit itself together and looked healthy. Other of the lacerations had begun to heal over, new pink flesh growing in the long gashes, around and between the sutures. It'd be days before he'd remove those.

Lulu began weeping. It annoyed him. No help at all.

"There, Kate. You're coming along. Soon you'll be healed up. Your eye made it through, thank God."

She said nothing.

"Too soon to pull out the stitches. That's going to be a bit painful, but we'll do it fast. Infection's mostly under control. You're winning, Kate."

She said nothing.

"They ask about you. Lot of fellows love you. Want to sit at your table again and enjoy that smile of yours. Half the army's patrolling out front, daring anyone to hurt you."

He began dabbing permanganate of potash into her wounds again, her forehead, cheeks, scalp, ear, neck, jaw. Her torn nose and lips remained too tender to touch. And he knew, as he studied them, that there'd be cruel scars there forever. And whole lattice works of scars elsewhere. His every stitch would leave its scar.

She must have seen it in his eyes as he studied her. She lunged for the looking glass on her bedside table, held it to herself, and screamed.

The sound paralyzed Santiago. The long, eerie wail, rising to shattering heights in that darkened bedroom only to wind down to a long desolate sob, pierced his soul.

She knew.

Payday. Jubal Peach leaned amiably into his bar, watching the throng. Ranch hands from all over had ridden into Miles for a last fling before hard weather set in. And the Buffalo Hump had become the place to lose their forty dollars, give or take a little for the parlor house girls. Wherever he looked in his green-and-cream club he saw sun-weathered drovers in leather vests and chaps, wearing blue or red or green neckerchiefs and big hats with the crown four-dimpled into the Montana peak. None was heeled, though he didn't doubt there'd be a saddle gun or two on the ponies crowding the hitch rails out front.

They mobbed Anna, who dealt faro happily while Eddie—one Eddie or another—manned the lookout stool above the game. She'd been flustered, with twenty or so bettors all plunking down chips. But this or that Eddie kept her straightened out and soon she dealt like a champ, enjoying those cowboy gazes that raked her shoulders and face and long, bare arms.

A stroke of luck, Jubal thought. Should have gotten her out at the tables years ago. She hadn't learned the edges yet, but that suited him fine. Let 'em win a bit, build up the trade now that The Stockman had shut down. That suited him, too, that quiet black hulk of a building around the corner on Sixth Street. He'd won. Soon as Kate healed up enough she'd flee Miles. It'd been a hard thing to do, but most of life's necessaries came hard. A few odds and ends still, do something about the law, and that would be it. Howitzer pressed for another sheet party, this time visiting the Tooles, but Jubal delayed.

Texans, that's what these drovers were. He listened to the soft accents. XT, over on the Powder. N-Bar, clear over at Grass Range. Swan, Niobrara, Flying D, all up from the Powder and Tongue. And from Texas. It pleased him. They didn't mind a little harrawing of Chinamen or a few games with Injuns. Not like the damned yankees around these parts, especially the blue-coat swaddies from Keogh.

Yes, Anna had become Queen of Miles City now, and it suited Jubal fine. Freed him, too. Nowadays he patrolled his other clubs instead of gluing himself to his faro game. Nowadays he could lean into the bar next to Howitzer and Walden and watch the coin change hands. Everywhere he saw greenbacks and gold and a few silver dollars, and knew he'd have it all by the end of the night. He chewed his unlit Cub and lifted his glass of amber syrup. With it he silently toasted the Queen of Miles City.

His front door swung open, billowing cold air into the close, hot club, and big men in buffalo coats entered, one after another, a dozen. Noncoms from Keogh, most of them fifty pounds heavier than the thin drovers from the ranches. They hung their curly black coats on elk-antler racks, revealing a sea of blue woolen winter tunics adorned with service chevrons just above the elbows.

Peach nodded to Howitzer. No love was lost between Texan cowboys, many of them Rebs, and the old sergeants, most of them Union Army vets. They'd brawled once or twice in here, demolishing more crockery and glassware and furniture and games than he cared to think about. Howitzer and Walden spread, and so did the other boys. The barkeeps looked to their scatterguns, always the most effective brawl-stoppers.

Always touchy, he thought. Get too rough and you lose trade. Be too lax and you lose profits. His boys knew that.

The noncoms filtered to the bar.

"Evening, gents. Make yourself comfortable."

The horde of blue-coats sifted in around him, bellying up and ordering red-eye. The very sight of that blue wool stirred black rage in Peach, but he checked it with a smile. Whenever men like this closed around him he went cold. He downed the syrup but it didn't calm him.

A trim, weathered sergeant major stood beside him, sipping red-eye thoughtfully, his lips puckering at the taste of that harsh booze. Peach knew the man. Patsy Gavin.

"Where you from, Peach?"

"Just about everywhere, sir."

"From the South."

"Oh, long time ago. Anaway, I'm up here now."

"Wearing sheets," the sergeant said so softly Peach wasn't sure he heard.

Peach laughed.

"These gents don't take kindly to cutting up a beautiful lady."

This sergeant was speaking so softly his voice scarcely carried to Peach's ear. In the hubbub no one caught the tenor of this conversation, least of all Howitzer and the boys. Peach sweated, smiled, and weighed meanings.

"It was unmannerly, anaway," Peach replied. "Doesn't sound southern to me, doing that to a lady."

"Exactly," whispered the sergeant major. "Don't know that the Klan has much against Chinamen, either. The boys here think maybe it wasn't really the Klan."

"No one knows. You fellows want sport? I can deal faro for you."

"No, you stay here," the sergeant said. It sounded amazingly like a command to Jubal.

"Over there at our noncom barracks we heard the news, Miss Kate all cut up and bleeding and her place shut down. And old Boris—a cossack colonel, you know—old Boris shot in cold blood. Now, that upset some of these old three-stripers some."

The sergeant major's words slid out so softly that Peach strained to hear. The sergeant shoved his glass toward the barman, who poured another round.

"We love our Kate."

"Well, we all do, Sergeant. Why, she's a legend around here. Hate to see her hurting. I suppose she'll go east now, get healed up."

"We thought maybe to take up a collection for Kate. But that don't cut ice. So we thought maybe to send flowers. But Peach, there ain't no flowers at the end of October in this country. Then we got to talking funerals. You know. Time for funerals. Like that one she threw for you. The boys are still talking about that one, Peach."

It worried Peach a bit, people putting together Kate's fancy funeral for him and Kate's subsequent injuries.

"Anaway, we joke back and forth, Kate and me. She gives me fancy funerals."

"And you wear sheets. We thought we'd look for sheets tonight. Mind if we start here?"

"Private property, sergeant. Of course, you're welcome—"

" 'Private' don't cut ice with the army. Where are your sheets, Peach?''

"Just because I'm southern that doesn't mean—"

"Exactly, Peach. Army's been dealing with the Klan down there for years. Ever since the Force Acts. The boys tell me this thing here, it don't look southern at all.''

The wiry sergeant major still spoke so quietly that not even the barmen hovering a few feet away heard. Peach sweated.

"I agree, Sergeant. Those Celestials—"

"Peach. I'm putting all your clubs off limits. I got Colonel Wade to sign it this afternoon. From now on the enlisted men can go to The Stockman, The Grey Mule—you got the games there but not the place itself—or the dives. I'm thinking most of the boys will go to The Stockman. Always did like it, and Miss Kate.''

"You got no reason, Sergeant."

"Army's unreasonable, Peach."

"You'll hurt my trade. I've always been good to your boys."

"Sheets," whispered the sergeant major. He nodded and the whole crowd of noncoms shrugged into their buffalo coats and walked out. Gaming paused. Cowboys stared.

The Stockman, Jubal thought, after wrestling his fear and rage back. Find a front man to run it and make an offer. Or maybe just take it. Kate, he thought, was about to go east. Maybe down the river. Damn the army.

Chapter 18

Monk Jeffords, the paunchy president of the bank, caught Santiago at his sheriff's office the next day.

"How's Miss Dubois?" he asked.

"Coming along."

"Is it possible to see her? On business?"

"No, I'm afraid not."

Jeffords pondered a moment. "Could you convey a message? There's a party interested in buying The Stockman. I've been authorized to offer five hundred dollars for her equity in it."

"Who?"

"Confidential, Toole."

"Does the five hundred amount to her equity in the building?"

"That's confidential, too, Santiago."

"Is she in danger of defaulting on her mortgage?"

"Sorry, Toole."

"I won't pass the word to her, Jeffords. Not now. That's a medical verdict."

The banker stared unhappily. "Could you give me some indication of when—"

"Not for a long time—if ever. That's a hell of a proposal. I don't know what her equity is, but it's many times five hundred."

"My party thought he was doing her a favor, Toole."

"Some favor, Jeffords. Tell him I said no."

"We'll approach her directly, then."

"The sheriff's office will shoot on sight anyone entering that building, Jeffords. And as a doctor I'll testify in court that she is not capable of making large decisions at the moment."

Something retreated in Jeffords's brown eyes and he lumbered out onto Main Street. Santiago fumed. Taking advantage of an injured, broken woman like that. He had a good idea who'd made the offer, and that made him even madder.

Kate's young body healed itself day by day, but her mind and soul had declined into a state that alarmed Santiago. He had some small knowledge of the healing of bodies but felt helpless to deal with broken hearts and black emotions. She would, he knew, probably sign any document thrust before her by a threatening male, such as Jeffords. He thought of going to Pericles Shaw with a petition to act as her conservator, but he decided against it for the time being. She seemed rational, not mad.

He grabbed his black pigskin bag and hurried to The Stockman on the first of his twice-daily visits. Somehow he had to talk life back into her, life and hope and love. His enemy was that looking glass. Sometimes, in the middle of his visits and his efforts at cheer, she'd pick it up and stare and die before his eyes. He felt like smashing the thing, but in fact it was an ally of sorts, because it recorded day by day the healing of her face. The purple and yellow and angry reds had vanished. The small dimples, left by the sutures when he'd pulled them, filled. The swelling receded. The scar tissue that cocked her left eye seemed less angry. The mirror showed her all these things but also showed her a devastated, scarred, twisted face, with lips torn into a strange grimace and a nose uneven and twisted.

He found her sitting up in bed, staring at the overcast November sky. The need for her to be in bed had long vanished but she clung to it, rarely getting up.

"Kate, put your wrapper on. It's time for you to be up and walking and keeping your muscles trim, lass."

She stared at him. He found her wrapper and held it open for her. Reluctantly she wheeled out of bed and slid into it.

"Now then, Kate, we'll walk. And I want you to walk every minute you can. Walk until you're too tired and then walk more, lass."

He took her hand and led her around and around, while Lulu watched solemnly. Kate didn't resist, and that worried him more than if she'd fought him about it.

"Have you given some thought to the future, Kate?"

"No."

"It's time. Time to think of reopening. There's a hundred cowboys and a regiment of soldiers out there pulling for you, eager to come in again. They love you, Kate."

"Not when they see me."

"Oh, they'll stare. And blink a time or two. And then settle down at your table, waiting for that smile, and those gray eyes of yours to notice them."

"No. It won't be like that."

"Kate. There's more to beauty than flesh."

She didn't respond to that.

"In any case, lass, we've all got to go on living. We didn't ask to be born, did we? But we've got to manage. We have to pick ourselves up and go on."

"Why?"

"Because there's breath in us. Because God wants us to."

"I'm not a believer."

"Well then, because your mind works, your lungs work, your heart pumps, and you want food and love and want to give what you have to others."

"Those are all just words."

"By the time we're middle-aged, lass, we all have scars on our faces. Some have the lines of laughter, some have the crinkle around their eyes of tenderness and love. But some have a scowl stamped on them, heavy creases they made themselves. You've got a chance to make a sweet, fine face, lass. You smile now and all those cowboys will toss their hats in the air. You care for them, know them all by name as you did, those eyes of yours'll fascinate them, and they'll find mysterious love in them. Think on it, Kate!"

"I'm tired and I want to lie down now."

In a moment she had settled herself back in her bed and was staring up at him blankly. He sat down on the edge of it, took her cold hand, and held it tight.

"It's will now, Kate. The will to live. You have a whole long life left. I won't say the scars are pretty. They'll shock people. Some will turn their gaze away. But you have life and health left. Know what'll happen when you reopen? Men'll take your hands, kiss them, and cry."

"I wouldn't like that at all."

"Kate. You're beautiful. Utterly beautiful."

She wept.

He held her hand a while more, feeling helpless and small in the face of terrible troubles, and then slid out into a blustery cold morning. He had patients waiting, he knew, but chose instead to head for the bank. Inside, he bulled through the low walnut gate partitioning the rear, while tellers gaped and glanced at the badge glinting on his breast. He found Jeffords in his dark office, the November gloom driven back by a single lamp, and settled himself in the chair across from the bank president.

"I must say, Toole. You've barged in—"

"When is Kate's next mortgage payment due?"

Jeffords looked vexed. He rolled mustache tips in his fingers.

"How much is it, Jeffords?"

The man's brown eyes studied his desk, his gaze sliding toward the floor, the lamp. "I can't really divulge—"

"She's not able to deal with anything. All right, Jeffords. Since you won't tell me, I'm going to Pericles Shaw. I'm going to ask for a temporary guardianship on my diagnosis as a physician. You're going to be dealing with me, not her. If you—or whoever you represent—make any moves at all, I'll meet you in court, I'll obtain injunctions, and I'll enforce them."

Jeffords sighed softly and steepled his hands. "December 31, next annual payment. Two thousand dollars."

"What's her equity?"

"I'd have to check. She's repaid around half of an eight-thousand-dollar loan. Repaid half the principal, plus eight percent.''

''Five hundred dollars, Jeffords! You tell Peach that Sheriff Toole will break his neck if he tries it.'

''You have no proof. . . .''

''I have no proof he cut her face, either. But I'll get it.''

''Her assets are gone, Toole. The buy-out's a generous offer.''

''She's got more assets, Jeffords, than you ever knew existed. Tell that to Peach. And you can tell Peach she'll be reopening one of these days, when she's better.''

''I thought you said she's incompetent.''

''Temporarily.''

Jeffords glared. ''This bank will protect its investment. We've got lawyers, too. We'll challenge this guardianship you propose. She's six weeks from default, Toole, and we won't be waiting around. In the meanwhile I'll see if I can arrange for the buyer to offer her approximately her equity. Guardian or not, you can't wriggle out of that. Shaw would have to approve.''

The portly man stood dismissively, and Santiago wheeled out. He'd gotten key information he needed. He had six weeks to lift Kate's spirits, get her to reopen, and hope she could come up with a mortgage payment. It didn't seem promising.

He wondered why he cared so much. Why so many men in Miles cared so much. Would they recoil from her when she reopened? Could she find the courage to sit once again at that faro table, with her face creased by scars that twisted her mouth, ruined her nose, latticed her forehead, trenched her neck, and left a hump of pink scar and a jagged valley across the corner of her left eye and down? It seemed too much for any woman to bear.

Jubal Peach didn't like this at all. He needed The Stockman, now that his other clubs were off limits to enlisted men. Just when he had everything in hand at last that sergeant major had lowered the boom on him. Trade had fallen at once. The soldiers earned a pittance—thirteen dollars a month—but Keogh had eight hundred of them and it added up. The cowboys earned more but they were few, and not inclined to venture out much in winter. Peach could see it everywhere. Immediately receipts fell off; Anna's faro table drew fewer sports. The other clubs suffered. And The Grey Mule, which he didn't own, boomed.

Why was life like that? It had always been thus. He'd gotten his fingertips on his goal, touched it, only to lose it once again. Restlessly he pulled his narcotic from a drawer in his desk and guzzled, waiting for instant heaven to steal through him. He could think better when his soul was floating. He corked the syrup again and jammed the bottle back. Time to order another four dozen from Hartford, he thought.

The opiate stole his anger away, and that made it better. Anger never helped. He'd been in a rage ever since Jeffords told him that no one could see Kate; that Toole would act as guardian for Kate. It wasn't right, doctor and sheriff in the same body, sheriff enforcing medical opinion. That's all it was, opinion. Kate had Toole's sympathy, and now Toole was talking about her competence. A few cuts on the face and he called her incompetent. Some doctor. A politician, actually. Blocking his purchase of The Stockman.

Jeffords had suggested offering full equity. Peach shoved his Eventual cigar around, weighing it. A lot of money. He had it, but he hated to part with it. She might not sell even at that, just to spite him. She might let the mortgage default, and it'd take months before he could get his hands on it. It annoyed him that he didn't know her state of mind, that Toole kept her hidden away up in her apartment, that she didn't act, didn't put The Stockman up for sale and leave Miles. It'd been six weeks now, and she was probably as healthy as a new filly. Nothing but a few scratches. Toole's threat— conveyed by Jeffords—irked him: anyone entering The Stockman would be shot on sight. A bluff.

He spun the combination on his safe and swung the gray-enameled steel-plate door open. A thousand dollars. He'd offer her that, in cash. He swung the door shut swiftly. He wondered whether to hang on to that Klan sheet in there or burn it. The thing had uses, but it presented dangers. He decided to hang on to it for a while. The others had been wrapped in oilcloth and stuffed in a fox den in a bluff up the Tongue three miles. Safe enough. Might be useful again.

He slid the hundreds into a manila pay envelope and wandered out into the saloon. Hardly any sports around, but the evening hadn't started. He found Howitzer consuming wealth in a corner, stuffing himself with dills and boiled eggs. He nodded, and Howitzer abandoned half a pickle and followed Peach into the office again. Peach shut the door.

"We're going visiting. Going to buy out Kate. Where's Toole? When does he visit her?"

"Mornings after his rounds, and right about now."

"We gotta wait. You go watch. See if he's in there."

"How'm I supposed to know that?"

"Do it. And figure out how we can get in. Front door's locked and Toole uses a key on the back."

"Skeleton key. I can pick it in ten seconds."

"Anaway, find where Toole is."

Howitzer nodded, picked pickle from his teeth with a silver toothpick, and vanished. Peach occupied himself by drafting two copies of a bill of sale, leaving numbers blank. He'd have to remember to bring a nib and an ink bottle in his satchel.

Howitzer didn't return for an hour.

"He's been there, looks like. He's at his house now. Chowing down."

"Where's Garrison?"

"Who knows?"

"Find him! We got to know."

That turned out to be easy. Ten minutes later Howitzer reported that the marshal was supping at Professor Bach's Restaurant around the corner, served by the Turk, Ugurplu, who used to work for Kate.

Delightful news. Jubal Peach slid into his black woolen greatcoat and the pair plunged into a black, bitter November evening with air that smelled like iron. Cutting through the block, past dark walls, they arrived at the rear door of The Stockman.

"I'll knock. That maid'll answer. Business call. Anaway, when I get in, you stay down here and watch. Don't shoot Garrison if you can help it. Just buffalo him. Hold him off. I'll do a little business and that'll be it."

He hammered on the dark door and eventually a dim face peered out through the wavy, bubbled glass.

"Go away," said the woman from within.

"Come to see Miss Kate on a little business is all."

"Miss Dubois is not available."

"Well, you go ask if she'll talk with Jubal Peach. Just good business."

The woman stared and then shuffled up the dark stairs, her dim figure vanishing in the gloom. Swiftly Howitzer slid a small steel jimmy into the lock, wiggled it a few times, pulled back a bit, and then flipped the bolt. They slid in and didn't wait for the maid. Howitzer closed the door behind them and posted himself in the blackened vestibule, almost invisible from outside. Peach cleared his throat and trotted up the creaking treads, whistling, making himself known.

The maid waited at the top, holding a small revolver.

"Go away."

"Naw, I'm just going to offer Miss Kate some money."

"You heard me. I'll shoot."

"Naw. You just wait a minute."

He barged past her, knowing she wouldn't nerve herself to do it. He'd never been up there. The stairs opened upon a parlor. Beyond lay a lamp-lit room, probably Kate's bedroom. To one side lay a kitchen, an alcove, and utility rooms.

"Miss Kate," Peach called from the parlor. "Peach here. Have a little business."

Nothing. He contemplated barging into her private room and decided against it. He wanted a signature.

"Miss Kate. I just want to talk a little. Have a fine offer for you."

"Please leave," Kate said.

"Well, I will in a moment. I'd like to buy the place. I've

got a thousand in cash here in my satchel, and bills of sale. That's a nice offer, Kate. Get you started somewhere.''

She greeted that with silence. He couldn't see her in the other room and had no idea how she'd reacted to his proposal. He knew she wouldn't come out. Not with those scratches.

''That's a bad thing, what the Klan did. Hurt you like that. But you can trust me. I won't even look. Come on out, Miss Kate, and we'll have us a talk. We need a talk. Seems things went downhill between us after that joke, that burying you did on me.''

Silence.

''I'm fearsome sorry about what the Klan did. Doing that to a beautiful woman like you. Those ruffians should be tarred and feathered. I ought to offer a reward.''

Kate said nothing. Jubal cased the place. The maid stood dourly, weapon in hand but defeated. She'd never pull that trigger.

''You can stay here a while, mebbe the end of the year. I'll not charge rent. I just want the club, is all. Seems a good solid outfit you got together. I wanted to offer a fair price, not take advantage. Big mortgage I've got to assume. Monk Jeffords says fine, if Miss Kate agrees. I take it you're thinkin' on it in there. That's all right. Go ahead and think. Those scratches don't bother me none, and you can talk here. I'll set me down and wait.''

''Leave.''

Peach settled into a horsehair easy chair. Kate's parlor had been done right handsome. Flocked blue wallpaper, Brussels carpet, cream enamel on the fluted woodwork.

''You've been asked to leave,'' said the maid. ''Since you won't, I'll go get help.'' She turned and started down the stairwell.

Into Howitzer's grasp.

''Miss Kate. I'm just going to settle here until you come on out and talk. We'll just have a little talk.''

''I will not sell to you—ever.''

''Why, Miss Kate, you've got no cause.''

"Cigars," she replied. "You smell the same in a white sheet as you do now."

It jolted him. "Lots smell of cigars, Miss Kate."

"Only one wanted to put me out of business. Destroy me. You succeeded. I am destroyed."

"Anaway, I have an offer you can't refuse. In six weeks you end up with nothing. But here's a thousand dollars, enough for a couple of years somewhere. I'll throw in a train ticket."

She didn't reply. He toyed with the possibility of killing her, not liking it. Cigar breath. He should have thought of that. Not that it mattered. That wasn't proof.

That's when she appeared at the doorway, in her white wrapper, and that's when he wanted to look anywhere else, anywhere except at the ghastly ruin of a beautiful face.

Chapter 19

She watched him try to look at her. He couldn't manage it. She stood quietly at the doorway, letting him try. His gaze flicked up to her from his chair and then skidded swiftly away, darting to the lamp, the Brussels carpet, the fluted creamy woodwork, the gilt-framed oil paintings on the walls. Anywhere.

He couldn't look, and he stared at his satchel.

"You see."

"You're beautiful, Miss Kate. You're just as beautiful as ever. I must say."

"I'm told that beauty rises from within."

"That's right, Kate. Within. Comes right through in a woman's smile, her way of looking at the world."

"That's right," she said. "From within. If a woman has a sweet nature, it shows. If she loves those around her, she somehow possesses beauty. If she listens, she becomes beautiful to the one who's talking. Isn't that right?"

"Right you are. Right you are."

She thought Peach sounded rattled. He stared at the carpet.

"But if a woman is sour, and has a mean tongue, then she's not beautiful, right?"

Peach nodded.

"If she's greedy, that shows in her nature, and destroys beauty."

Peach nodded.

"It's all in the soul. A woman can be born plain, but become beautiful in the eyes of her beholders."

"Well, anaway."

Peach clearly didn't know what to say, she thought.

"I think you need some of your syrup, Mr. Peach."

He looked relieved and pulled the bottle from his satchel, uncorked it, and swallowed a stiff dose, exhaling softly. "I'm a prisoner," he muttered.

"We all are prisoners."

"You have inner beauty, Miss Kate. No question about it. That Klan outfit, it didn't steal anything off you."

Peach made a great fuss of restoring the bottle to his satchel. His forehead was beaded with sweat, though an icy draft pervaded the parlor.

"All right," she said.

"All right what?"

"Let me see the bill of sale."

His gaze flicked up to her face again, but he couldn't hold it there and it fastened upon the satchel. "You saying . . ."

"Yes."

He fumbled in his bag and finally withdrew two sheets, filled with a fine copperplate. He thrust them at her, trying to meet her gaze, but he couldn't.

"I'm hard to look at, Mr. Peach."

"You got inner beauty," he croaked.

She settled down next to the lamp and read. She would surrender her equity in the building. And include the saloon furnishings, games, and tables. He would pay her a thousand dollars cash. He would assume her debt to the bank. She would agree not to remain in Custer County. She would agree not to open a new club in Miles City. She would agree to leave by December 1.

"December 1."

"Well, that's just to give me possession."

"You don't want me upstairs while you run the club below."

"Well, I thought it might . . . dampen things."

She smiled, feeling the scars pull at her lips and twist them into a grimace.

"I would have two weeks, then."

"Well, that's negotiable. You still feel you can't travel, why, I could give a little extra. . . ."

"Very well."

"You mean you agree? You'll sign?"

She nodded.

He waited. She realized he hadn't seen her nod, with his gaze riveted to the floor.

"Yes."

He scrambled up and began yanking his ink pot and nib from the satchel. He handed them to her, staring at her graceful white hands.

"A blotter."

He found one. She dipped the nib in the ink and scratched her name. Katherine Dubois. Twice. And the date. She blotted it.

"Well, then. Anaway, here's the cash."

Peach pulled out a packet of bills, licked his thumb, and began counting. All hundreds.

"There, that's ten. Glad you decided. Now don't you worry about noise below. We'll be moving in—say, you got goods there? Whiskey and all?"

"Some."

"You going to throw that in?"

"A hundred dollars. Liquor stock, glasses, towels, and the rest."

"I'll give fifty."

She didn't reply. It didn't matter.

"Anaway, I'll get it to you."

She stood.

He scooped up one of the copies and left the other, and backed away.

"Glad we came to terms, Miss Kate," he said, and whirled out. He hadn't been able to meet her eyes.

A moment later Lulu burst up the stairs. "That man held me!" she announced.

Kate nodded.

"What have you done?" Lulu cried, seeing the agreement and the greenbacks.

"I'm tired, Lulu."

"You didn't!"

It wasn't important what Lulu thought.

"I'm going to find Dr. Toole! I'm going to tell him what happened. He won't permit this."

"Tomorrow. I'm tired now."

"You're not well. He took advantage of you. He threatened you."

"No." She walked back into her bedroom and its comforting darkness. From the window she could see across rooftops to Main Street. No one lingered there in the blustery wind. The club windows cast a dim amber glow out upon the rutted clay. A tumbleweed bobbed across the street, ghostly in the night. Still a raw prairie town, she thought. So different from Newport, Rhode Island.

She heard Lulu out in the parlor, gathering the cash and the paper, and sobbing. The soft snuffle disturbed Kate. She wished she could comfort the old woman. At her small escritoire she lit a cut-glass lamp, found a sheet of bond paper and her pens, and scratched a brief note. That would comfort Lulu. She blotted it and left it there.

She turned down the wick and the lamp blued out, smoking a moment, and then dark nestled around her. She headed toward the window again, delaying. In her young life she'd come a long way from the mansions of Newport, where she'd been inside and outside of a luxurious life. Miles City. She smiled, thinking of its rawness. Most of the buildings were made of logs, covered over now with planks and false fronts. Wooden cottages. Unpaved streets. Saloons and sporting places its principal business. A grand, ugly prairie stretching into wilderness. Cattle now. A few years ago, only buffalo and Indians and wolves.

Twenty-six. She felt health radiating through her young body. She could travel now. Her body had conquered the infection and had rebounded easily. Half a life lived, maybe a third of a life. Some people lived into their sixties these days.

She thought of Dr. Toole, who had come faithfully, healing her with his arts and sciences and holding her hand through the worst of it, when she'd lain bandaged, her eyes seeing nothing, the only reality endless, sharp pain, throbbing headaches, and desolation. He'd talked of picking up the threads of life, of struggling, of being caught in tribulations we can't help. Of God, of staying alive, of not surrendering. Of beauty of the soul, of the inner spirit. Of making lives, of adapting to the things we can't help. Of not letting terrible things crush us. He'd talked of all that, holding her hand, no doubt wondering if she'd heard.

She'd heard.

He'd talked of other things, too. Of being a younger son of an Irish nobleman and being banished for it, as was the custom. Of never seeing green Ireland again. Of coming to this brown place as an anodyne that hadn't worked. He had never stopped yearning, though he said his Mimi had helped him find a new life in these barren steppes of North America. A good, rewarding life.

She'd listened to that, too. His life hadn't gone the way he'd hoped and yet he'd struggled on, doing his best. He was telling her to do her best, to find the strength, somehow, to go on. She smiled at that. Santiago Toole had been a doctor of the soul and spirit as well as the body. She loved him for it, and wished she had some sort of faith so she might bless him with prayers. But she had no faith.

Out in the parlor only silence prevailed. Lulu had turned the lamp down and gone to bed in her alcove. Dear Lulu. She deserved more than she'd receive. Kate smiled. She settled down on her bed and found the blue bottle of laudanum Dr. Toole had left her for pain. Take five drops, he'd said. She poured one teaspoonful and swallowed it. And six more, until she had taken the last.

Santiago slumped in his rocking chair in his dark office, staring into the night. His whole self brimmed with black-

ness, and he had no light. He called it his Black Irish, and
Mimi had learned swiftly to leave him alone when those
times came. This one afflicted him worse than he'd ever
known and he took a perverse pleasure in it, in the pain of
it. He shouldn't have left the laudanum. She'd had screaming-
crazy headaches for a while, white pain, which only an opiate
helped. So he'd left her some.

But she'd have found other means. He realized, in that
moody dark, that he'd known all along, even though he hadn't
known. It had been something sensed rather than experienced. Even before this dawn when Lulu had summoned
him, tear-streaked, half-dressed, he'd known. Kate lay serene and cold, death reclaiming much of the beauty she'd
had cut out of her. He'd checked her heart and breath, read
her note giving the cash to Lulu and requesting burial in the
casket she'd bought. Then full of pity and rage and helplessness, he'd read the signed sales agreement. No judge could
stay the force of it now.

He'd lifted her up and wrapped a blue wool blanket around
her slender form and carried her across a dark November
dawn straight up Main Street, encountering no one but an
ash man. Her blond hair hung loosely, toyed with by the
eddying winds. He carried her gently, as he would a child,
not feeling the weight of her, only the coldness of her flesh.
Through the silent town of Miles City, past dead mercantiles
to Sylvane Tobias's living quarters at the rear of his business,
where he awakened the man. Sylvane appeared in a robe and
nightshirt, stared, and led Santiago silently through black
rooms to a place where a heavy table sat. Santiago hadn't
realized it but Lulu had followed, one pace behind, and as he
laid Kate down on that slab at last, Lulu stood beside him,
then crossed herself and knelt. They both knelt, muttering
hollow requiems to cover aching, naked chasms of the soul.

"Sylvane," he muttered at last. "She left a note asking to
be placed in that casket she bought—you know the one. Make
it day after tomorrow. And don't stint anything. Not anything. If you can't find a minister who'll bury a sporting
woman, I'll say words. I'm getting good at it."

Tobias nodded. "I'll dig up the casket. That face . . . My God, Santiago. Who can blame her?"

"Not man nor God."

Later, he'd hurried through most of his practice to shut the door at last and settle into his merciful rocker. Mimi squeezed his hand but said nothing. She chased away the curious, who came asking questions. Word of it bruited through town swiftly that day, and some who wanted news from him didn't get it. She admitted only Pericles Shaw, who discovered Santiago's mood, took the doctor's hand and held it, and left quietly.

That's how the afternoon faded away.

He'd thought to arrest Peach and all his men. Pound them. Some mayhem and murder of his own. But he lacked a shred of real evidence.

But in his soul he knew Peach had destroyed Kate Dubois. He knew it without proof, knew it in the worst possible way, without evidence, without the means to begin that solemn process called justice. He'd picked up a few scraps of rumor from friendly barmen; he'd tried to find out what he could about the Klan in the West from the Rocky Mountain Detective Association in Denver City. It all came to nothing. Kate had been savaged by parties unknown—officially.

Around ten that night Garrison rapped sharply on Toole's darkened door. Santiago ignored the marshal. Let him fight his own battles tonight, he thought, leaning back in his rocker in his office. But Garrison rapped harder and Santiago rose, blackly, to rebuke the younger man.

"Lynching. Need you," Garrison said. The town marshal had his Greener tucked under his arm. "Hurry."

"Who? Where?"

"The park. The cottonwoods. They're stringing up Peach, Howitzer, and that other, Clem Walden."

"Who?"

"More cowboys than I can count. And a few noncoms, all armed. They shooed me off."

Santiago whirled to the elk-antler coat track and slid into his black suit coat and a woolen greatcoat.

"My shotgun's at the jail."

"They got scatter-guns of their own."

"Who?"

"Noncoms. Patsy Gavin, sergeant major. He's got a double."

Santiago made a swift decision. "I'll go in unarmed."

"Don't."

But Santiago had plunged out, past the creaking gate in the picket fence, and hurried down Seventh toward Main. The park lay off of Park Street and extended to the river. The cottonwoods lay a few rods from the Sporting District.

"How'd it happen?"

"Mob busted into the Buffalo Hump. Caught Peach in his office and grabbed Howitzer and Walden at the bar."

"There's not a shred of evidence!"

"Don't slow 'em down none."

"I'll have them all on manslaughter."

"If you live."

The north wind bit at them, slicing into Toole's greatcoat and numbing his fingers. He'd forgotten gloves. Miles lay eerie in blackness, under a starless sky.

"Word got to the ranches fast."

"Seems so."

Far west on Main they saw the bob of lanterns. Santiago trotted, feeling time run out, feeling helpless to deal with this. He'd try the sergeant major first. The man breathed authority.

Closer now. He made out a mob, men and horses. Drovers in sheepskin coats and sealskin caps, wooly chaps, and boots. And buffalo-coated soldiers with blue kepis stationed around the perimeter. Beneath a stark black limb of a cottonwood three men sat on horses, thin white lines coiling from their necks to the limb above. He heard shouting, cursing, and then a gradual silence as the crowd folded back.

"Stop it! This is the sheriff!" Toole roared.

He puffed across the street and into the park.

Several noncoms lowered their scatterguns at him. He found Patsy Gavin, thin and gray and hard-eyed.

"Stop it!" Toole roared.

Gavin shook his head. "No. You go in there and you're dead, Sheriff."

"I'm unarmed, and I'm going in there."

He bulled past Gavin, but the sergeant's hand caught him.

"Toole. They were warned. If anything happened to Miss Kate, they'd be strung up. It happened."

"You have no proof. This is for the courts."

"There's proof."

But Santiago yanked loose, followed by Garrison, and shoved his way through to the doomed men. In the wavering lantern light Peach was slumped on a bay, hands tied, looking terrified. Howitzer trembled on a buckskin. He'd vomited down the front of his suit coat. Only Clem Walden sat quietly, silent and stolid.

"Sheriff! Stop them! Thank God you got here!" Peach screamed.

Drovers turned toward Santiago, swinging six-guns around.

"I'm unarmed and I'm taking these prisoners. Anyone interferes, he's obstructing justice."

"They ain't goin' anywhere, Toole. They been warned long ago, and we made promises." Luke Long said it. Ramrod of the XT.

"Law will handle this." He pushed through to the first horse, which supported Howitzer—for the moment.

"Drop it!" yelled someone behind him. He caught a glimpse of six drovers disarming Garrison.

"Do your duty!" yelled Long.

Cowboys stationed behind each horse smacked the animals with switches. The geldings shrieked, bucked, and plunged forward. The white ropes yanked their riders off their backs, and they dropped with sharp cracks. Then they swung in the lantern light, pendulums in the wind, their ropes creaking. A sudden hush fell, in the presence of death. Peach's noose had not snapped his neck and he gasped, bugeyed, tongue lolling, until finally something sighed out of him. Howitzer and Walden had died instantly and sagged upon their tethers, heads flopping.

Fury bit Santiago. "No evidence! You took the law into your hands! I'll have a grand jury and I'll—"

Some white billowing thing flew out of the mob and landed on him. He pawed at it, yanked at cloth, scraped it off until it deflated on the black clay. From the earth eye-holes gaped up at him. He retrieved it and shook it open. Klan sheet.

"Peach's," said Long. "In his safe. He was fetching another bottle from it when we busted in."

That didn't mollify Santiago one bit. "You were going to hang them anyway."

Patsy Gavin pushed his way forward. "Law's dumb sometimes, Sheriff. Men know what the law don't know."

"I'm reporting this to Colonel Wade and I'm recommending court-martial on murder charges."

From the edge of the lantern light a woman pushed through, a woman with bare shoulders and henna hair, not half a costume on a freezing night like this.

She reached the three dangling bodies.

"Oh, Jubal," she said, tears rising. "Oh, Jubal."

Sergeant Major Gavin pulled his buffalo coat off and wrapped it over her, pulling an arm over her shoulders. "Looks like you got a club to run, ma'am. You just run a square game and you'll be happy enough. You'll have army trade. I'll fix it at the fort."

"Oh, Jubal . . ."

The old sergeant slowly led her through the silent crowd and back to the Buffalo Hump, half a block away.

A desperate tiredness overwhelmed Santiago. "Do them the courtesy of a proper burial," he said. "Cut them down and take them over to Tobias."

"They don't get any grave but the river!" someone out in the darkness yelled. "They killed Miss Kate, no matter how you figure it happened!"

The drovers held Toole and Garrison prisoner while the bodies were cut down and packed over horses for the brief ride to the Yellowstone. Santiago watched what was left of

Jubal Peach and the others bob into the blackness. He felt too tired to say anything, too tired even for anger. Kate's death had drained every last bit of strength out of him, even before this.

"Sheriff. You and the marshal can go now," the sergeant major said. "Go ahead. Have your grand jury. Go tell Wade. Do what the law makes you do."

"Call me Dr. Toole, Sergeant," he said, and stumbled into the night.

Chapter 20

A blessed chinook had blown the cold out of Milestown, and by noon the thermometer stood at sixty. Santiago brushed his black frock coat and adjusted his vest. He unpinned his star and slid it into his pocket.

Mimi smiled at him, her face soft and olive and tender. She'd dressed in her black serge suit and carried a small white missal in her hand. She'd hugged him through his sleep, and he'd awakened to her tenderness that November morning.

They walked south on Seventh, feeling the balmy west wind and the fragile heat of the low sun. He steered her toward Tobias's, where they'd follow the great gleaming hearse once again as it wound its dark way up to the cemetery. There wouldn't be much of a crowd for a sporting woman like Kate. A few. Some of those cowboys, for sure.

Ahead he saw people on Main Street. Lots of people, and it irritated him a bit. When they reached the great artery of Miles City, they found crowds quietly lining the boardwalks.

"Santo, look!" Mimi exclaimed. She pointed at soldiers in dress blues, at parade rest about every fifty feet on both sides of the road. He stared, amazed. Every soldier wore a fresh-brushed blue tunic, britches with white bars down them, and spit-polished boots. The Fifth Infantry had come to Miles.

"Holy Mary!" he cried. Ahead, milling around Tobias's place, stood the Fifth Infantry Band, also in dress blues, its brass instruments glinting in the low sun. And ahead of it, in parade formation, all three troops of cavalry sat four abreast, every horse groomed and gleaming, sun dancing off brass buttons and McClellan saddles, with yellow ribbons streaming from the forelocks and tails and manes of each mount. Yellow ribbons dancing in the sun. Yellow ribbons everywhere.

Ahead, as far as he could see, infantrymen stood at parade rest every fifty feet. And ahead of the cavalry he discovered the cowboys, more cowboys than he'd ever seen in Miles at one time, cowboys with scrubbed faces, clean flannel shirts and bandannas of every hue, oiled saddles, groomed and brushed chaps, and glowing boots that had seen polish for the first time. And every mount beneath them had been groomed and combed and scrubbed until the whole cowboy contingent dazzled and glowed and shattered light like the Yellowstone casting sun off its shoulders.

"Holy Mary!" cried Santiago. Mimi caught his hand and held it as they walked into Tobias's.

They found Sylvane up on the glinting black hearse, looking grand and important, dressed in silk top hat and boiled shirt and swallowtail coat, holding the lines running out to Heaven and Purgatory, his white and gray drays. Within the hearse, visible through the oval cut-glass windows, lay the walnut box Kate had bought from Tobias not long before. But this time the box was not empty.

Santiago blessed himself.

"We've been waiting, Toole. You and Mimi take that carriage and we'll be off."

"Good Lord!" cried Santiago.

A carriage awaited them, drawn by Tobias's third dray, the black gelding Hell. In it sat Lulu, somberly clad, smiling wanly. Santiago slid into the front seat while Mimi clambered in from the other side, and at last they were ready. Santiago lifted the lines and waited for the hearse ahead to roll.

Sylvane, seeing that the moment had come, flicked his lines and the two drays pushed in their collars. The great black-and-nickel hearse rumbled out of its alley and onto Main Street, and turned west. At once the Fifth Army band, just ahead, snapped to attention. Santiago expected a dirge, but that wasn't what greeted him. They began with a smart roll of snare drums, which broke off abruptly into a sudden silence. And then, with brass to lips, they swung into "She Wore a Yellow Ribbon," the melody carried by eight trombones that pierced triumphantly through the crowds. The great parade had begun on a note of joy.

"Around her neck she wore a yellow ribbon. . . ."

And so they rolled down Main Street, the infantrymen at parade rest snapping to attention with a bright salute as the hearse rolled past, and then folding into the throbbing crowd that walked solemnly behind the hearse and the carriage.

"She wore it in the winter and on a summer day. . . ."

A thousand voices, along with those trombones, the brass and the drums. Oh Kate, lass. Oh Kate, he thought. If you could only see how they love you. . . . They've all come to say good-bye.

Ahead, the troops of cavalry snapped into a brisk walk four abreast, and the rattle of hooves reached back to those following the great hearse. They wore dress helmets, metal eagles gleaming on the front with yellow horsehair plumes catching sunlight.

All of Miles, he thought. All of Keogh, the whole garrison, eight hundred strong, save for a few left to man the place. They passed the commanding officer, Colonel Wade, at attention near the military bridge along with most of his junior officers, who folded into the great procession behind the hearse.

And when they asked her why she wore the ribbon,
She said it's for her lover who is far, far away. . . .

Holy Mary! thought Santiago. He had trouble seeing. The world had gone blurry.

They curled south toward the bluffs and still the soldiers in dress blues snapped to attention as the hearse passed, then folded into the growing crowd. On up the lonely road they went, all of Miles City in prayer-meeting best, all of Fort

Keogh, every cowboy within fifty miles, gaudy in green and blue and red shirts, wide-brimmed creamy hats, angora chaps, and bold bandannas, and some on silver-mounted saddles with great shining diamonds studding the skirts, all marching to say good-bye to Kate.

They rattled over rough ruts into the windswept cemetery, where tan grasses bobbed in the chinook breezes. Sylvane pulled up beside the open grave while the infantry band formed beside it and the flowing crowd gathered in a great arc. It was the very same hole where Kate had planted Peach, but Sylvane had taken away the headboard. And then, at last, the conductor lifted his baton and the plumed musicians began a slow, gentle version of "The Girl I Left Behind Me."

> Oh, that girl, that pretty little girl,
> That girl I left behind me.
> Oh, I'll laugh and cry till the day I die
> For the girl I left behind me.

At graveside stood the noncoms, spit and polish, their blues weighted down with service stripes, medals, gold lanyards, and gleaming sabers in polished sheaths. Six of them opened the rear door of the hearse and gently slid the dark box out and lowered it reverently into its nest in the hard clay of Custer County. Commanding them was the slim sergeant major, Patsy Gavin.

Santiago gaped.

"You wish to say a few words, Dr. Toole?" asked the old sergeant.

Santiago steadied himself, not knowing what to say. He hadn't expected this. Before him in a great arc stood the largest crowd ever gathered in Miles City. Probably a thousand soldiers, cowboys, and railroad men, and virtually every civilian in the county, adding another thousand. Plus a solemn contingent of Northern Cheyenne, dressed in their finest ceremonial skins. Their presence was a far more eloquent eulogy than anything he could think of.

"We've come to say good-bye to a lady!" Santiago cried,

hoping his words would drift outward. "The girl we left behind us!"

He felt uncomfortable, facing that vast sea of expectant faces, waiting for him to do justice to Kate Dubois.

"There's nothing to say that hasn't been said by your presence here, this parade, this band, this farewell. Each one of you loved Kate Dubois."

He led them, then, through the Twenty-Third Psalm and a brief prayer.

The sergeant major saw he was done and barked a brief command that pierced out into the silence. Every infantryman present formed a long blue line, and began to pass by Kate's grave. Each one had a flower that he dropped upon the casket—not a real flower in November, but one he'd fashioned from some bit of bunting and ribbon—and when they had finished the cavalry troopers added the yellow ribbons from their mounts and the cowboys and the gandy dancers all dropped their paper roses and forget-me-nots. And when they'd all passed by Santiago peered into that hole and found a miracle. Over the walnut box a great rainbow leaped up toward the dark sky.

When at last all this was completed, a lone trumpeter with a black band wrapped around his arm stepped out and played taps. A low brass sun caught the trumpet until it blazed, a living thing. Those long soft notes hung in the clear, sweet prairie air, and then drifted softly into the distant, lonely hills and died there.

The wind had turned cold.

"Ah Kate, lass," he muttered. "You did us proud."

Santiago held Mimi's hand, while mourners came to the grave for a final moment and then drifted on down the hill.

"Santo, how they loved her," Mimi said. "She gave them dreams."

About the Author

RICHARD S. WHEELER is the Spur Award-winning author of many Westerns. *Deuces and Ladies Wild* is the third in his Santiago Toole series, which includes *Incident At Fort Keogh* and *The Final Tally*. Mr. Wheeler makes his home in Big Timber, Montana.

G. CLIFTON WISLER

************ *presents* ************

THE DELAMER WESTERNS